Praise for *Colossus*:

"Greg Leunig opens new worlds for readers in this page-turning novel. History and myth and sci-fi come together in a cavalcade of awesomeness--and delivered so smoothly that you won't want to put the book down. A promising new voice on the ever-changing speculative-lit scene."

— Teague von Bohlen, author of *Flatland* and *The Pull of the Earth,* and fiction editor of *The Copper Nickel.*

"From the gritty streets of future Floridian cyber-sprawl to the magical ruins of far-off Rhodes, Greg Leunig's cyberpunk adventure debut grabs hold of genre tropes and wrenches them into new, otherworldly shapes. Part Neuromancer, part National Treasure, Colossus is one hell of a ride."

— Brandon Getz, author of *Lars Breaxface, Werewolf in Space* and *Stop Me If You've Heard This One Before.*

"A pulpy thriller with a classical twist, COLOSSUS shines with its cast of ragtag characters racing against secret societies in an all-too-plausible corporate-controlled future."

— Erica L. Satifka, author of *How to Get to Apocalypse and Other Disasters*

COLOSSUS

GREG LEUNIG

Denver, Colorado

Published in the United States by:

Spaceboy Books LLC
1627 Vine Street
Denver, CO 80206

www.readspaceboy.com

First printed September 2022

ISBN-13: 978-1-951393-17-5

For my girls:

My wife, Bailey Ross, who has always supported me and helped me muster the motivation to work on this book on weekends when I'd rather be gaming.

Our dogs, Juno and Zelda, who ensure I never have to snack alone in the middle of the night.

SELINA KAN

Selina Kan stepped out of the shadows and into the stale white halogen light that bathed the corner of 5th and Main. Humidity so thick it might've been fabric – a stiff polyester – clung to her skin, soaked her grey cotton shirt all the way through, dripped off her synth-leather duster like rain. Her hair was wet with it, her shoes squished on the ground. It might as well have been pouring rain in Jacksonville that night. The thick atmosphere made a mosaic of the full moon above-not one star was visible.

In the distance, in the corporate high rises just outside the city center, Selina could hear noise. Bustle. The distant base of booming music intermingled with the shriek of faraway sirens. Nightlife in full swing, for those with the money for it.

Not here, though. Nobody had money here in the old city center, except for Mauricio. And, soon, her.

Her right hand rested comfortably in her pocket; her fingers coiled around the grip of a small stun gun. Her left, in her other pocket, worried at a small data-drive, the hard plastic of it slick from the sweat and the humidity.

Mauricio was coming. Strolling the down the street without a care in the world. He always took his time. Putz. Hadn't been police in Jacksonville for decades, and the corporate cops didn't bother with downtown – no money in protecting the lowlifes and the gutter walkers. He was acting like a 20th century gangster, playing it cool. Not someone out fencing illegal data-dumps from corporate R&D databases; just a pedestrian out for a leisurely stroll. In one of the most dangerous parts of the Florida metro-sprawl. But there wasn't anyone around for him to fool.

He was tall, Mauricio, and maybe he didn't have as much concern as Selina because he was also built like an ox. He wore a poly-mesh workout suit, bright blue, cut off at the knees and shoulders. She knew he was strapped. He didn't bother trying to blend in, wearing the dark greys and blacks of the rest of the city; didn't believe in it, he would say whenever she asked him. It would get him killed one day.

Maybe today. Two hooded figures followed Mauricio, about twenty paces back, but gaining ground. She was about to step forward and warn him, when she heard a voice from an alley behind her.

"Hey, sweetheart."

She spun to see a third hooded figure looming towards her. A man — bearded, dark hair. Ratty pants, grey; hooded vest, grey. Bright blue tattoos, nonsense words and strange swirls, sharp on both of his exposed arms. The man tossed a knife from his right hand to his left, and back again, grinning, reveling in the motion of it.

Great. The Bermuda Gang. 'Mudes. The weirdest damn gang to populate the Florida metro-sprawl, or really any of the American South. Heavy into psychedelics, and big fans of knifing people in dark alleys. This guy would be glad to loot her corpse, but the killing would be what got him off.

Before the 'Mude could react, she pulled the stun gun out of her pocket, levelled it at him. He grinned wider, the psycho, and she wasn't taking any chances. Who knew what sort of shit flowed hot through his veins? Amps, combat stims, any of the smorgasbord of PCP descendants. She squeezed the trigger hard, and again, and again.

Three micro-darts buried themselves in the grinning maniac's belly, each meting out several pulses of electricity in quick succession. He dropped, still grinning but unconscious.

She heard the harsh crack of gunpowder and turned just in time to see Mauricio go down, a knife in his shoulder and his throat cut. He fired his old handgun again, the bullets going wide. One of the two hooded figures was still up, and ambling towards her. As it drew nearer, Selina could see blue tattoos on exposed arms.

She bit her lip, hard, until she could taste blood. Mauricio was dead, the cocky bastard. And she was still holding a drive full of stolen corporate secrets for a buyer that only Mauricio knew. He had her money in his pockets, and there was just one jacked up ganger with a knife between them. Might be more nearby, but she was hungry, and she had plenty of ammo left.

She flipped the dial on her stun gun to lethal, and it buzzed. A soft voice warned her that lethal force mode was now engaged. "You heard that, right?" Selina said, leveling the gun at the figure up ahead.

The 'Mude stopped. Hesitated.

Selina took the cue and stepped forward. Sweat poured down her back. She had a brief panic attack when she thought the gun was slipping out of her grasp. She played it cool, though, advancing like a terminator. The last 'Mude decided she wasn't worth the trouble, turned and ran across the street, into another alley.

Selina exhaled slowly, looking around. Nobody else nearby to capitalize on her distraction, and none of Mauricio's dealers had come running at the sound of exploding gunpowder. Good. Wouldn't want them getting agitated when she looted his corpse.

As she knelt beside him, she realized he wasn't quite dead yet. He tried to speak, but the blood flowing steady through the hole in his throat just burbled, and no words came. He tried to reach out for her, but couldn't seem to muster the strength to do more than lift his arm a few centimeters off the ground.

"Sorry, compadre," she said, reaching into the pockets of his workout suit. "Biz is biz, and anyway, I told you over and over you needed to blend in around here."

She found a lighter, a pack of smokes. Left those. And then in the other pocket, pay-dirt. The cred-drive, a small stick pre-loaded with credits. She took the data-drive out of her pocket and slid it into his. A deal's a deal, she thought. She didn't want that thing anyway, if WalCo decided it was worth their while to come looking for the hacker that stole their secrets in downtown Jacksonville. No, thank you.

Still crouched, she heard a noise from behind, a quiet scuffling, and spun to see the 'Mude she'd put down mere moments ago, on his feet and stumbling towards her. Obviously disoriented still, but almost on her, knife point sharp and glimmering and hungry for blood, her blood, hungry to bring it out hot and steaming into this sticky, sweltering Florida night. Her gun arm whipped forward almost of its own volition, and she put five in his belly and chest, beside the other three, these unloading the full amperage of their micro-batteries all at once, a flood of electricity coursing through the ganger, his body spasming once, and then dropping again. This time there was the smell of singed flesh. The man was dead.

She shuddered, stood. Mauricio's old 9 millimeter, practically an antique but without the value, still rested on the sidewalk beside its erstwhile owner. She hesitated. Didn't care much for old shit, but figured she could find a use for the weapon. A gun was a gun after all, and in this world you could never have too many. She grabbed the heavy metal thing and pocketed it, before disappearing back into the shadows of the street, and making her way quietly home.

NAGASH JENSEN

Gash felt himself flush with anticipation. The woman had just peeled off the last of his socks, sucking each toe in turn. She was lithe, voluptuous, raven hair halfway down her chest, legs for days. Everything he'd ever wanted in a woman. She rose to her feet, pushing off the sofa that she'd just moments ago pushed him into. Haloed in the bright light of the patio door behind her, she looked... well, she looked like an angel. A lingerie-clad angel. A porn angel. She began a little dance, her fingers starting to work their way around to the clasp of the bra on her back.

Outside, palm trees swayed modestly in the wind, ocean waves crashing just below the outcropping on which the mansion had been built. A soft breeze rustled the woman's hair and slid catlike along his naked thighs and torso, tickling the hairs on his legs and arms.

"Do you know what I want to do to you first, big boy?" she asked.

And then, before she could say what she wanted to do to him, everything went black. No more breeze, no more ocean, no more woman.

He yanked the cumbersome apparatus off his head. Trodes

caught in his hair, and the thick stalk of cables attaching it to the old dentist's chair on which he sat got tangled on an arm. Before he could get untangled, an old Jamaican woman stuck her head through the door into the tiny casket of a room, saying something in an accent too thick and words too fast for him to follow.

"What the hell?" he growled. "She was just about to tell me what she wanted to do to me first."

Someone outside pushed her aside. A younger Jamaican man stuck his head in. "You cred-drive run out o' funds already, mon. No freebies here, ya' deadbeat."

"I thought it was 20 credits to get off, so I say again, what the hell?"

"20 credits for 15 minutes, deadbeat," the young man said, gesturing at the poster on the far wall of the little stall, the same one plastered on the walls outside the shop. Gash had only paid attention to the woman – a blonde with unusually large implants – and the big red text. "20 credits for the steamiest Real-D in Jacksonville," it said. Now Gash read the fine print, which did indeed specify 20 per 15 minutes.

"Who the hell reads the fine print?" Gash grumbled.

"Get outta here, deadbeat," he tossed the little stick at Gash, and it landed in his lap.

He tapped it against his PCom, and the holo-display read: "$0." Damn. They took him for what little he had left. He slid it into his pants pocket, grabbed his long black coat and dingy old hat from the coat hanger on the wall, and stepped out of the stall sporting a raging hard-on. Past two dozen other stalls he limped, and into the front desk area.

The carpet had once been white, the walls painted a sort of pre-historic bone beige; but now a thick patina of filth coated the place, reducing everything to shades of grey. Vending machines for smokes, candy bars, and beers lined the far wall; three-fourths empty, these now held nothing but weird off-brand shit that patrons had been ignoring for half a decade. The pretty young receptionist was slotting out someone else's cred-drive. His time must've been up, too. She looked up at him and winked, mouthed the words "come back soon."

Not fucking likely.

He stepped out and into a deluge. Florida was in full-on monsoon season, and the weather ranged from 110 percent humidity to full-on Biblical rainfall. Evidently, tonight they were slated only for the latter. His hat and the long cut of his coat sloughed off water by the buckets, but in about ten seconds the rain soaked Gash to the core.

He fumbled in his jacket pocket, managed to produce a half-empty pack of Marlboros. Squeezed a soggy one out, and tried to light it in the sheltered space between his hand, his mouth, and the brim of his hat. No luck. Grimacing, he let it drop to the sidewalk in front of the Real-D Parlour, and stepped out into the throng that pulsed through the streets of Jacksonville.

This part of the city, referred to by the locals as "Limbo," was always packed. A few blocks over, downtown would be almost deserted. Only thing that place was good for was crime. Drug deals, espionage deals, black market wares deals – pretty much any kind of deals that would land a dealer on the wrong side of a major corporation with its own sec-team. Plus of course the muggings, murders, and rapes that accompanied such places. A few blocks in the other direction were the work-towns, and these would be busy, but not too busy. Corporate housing, shopping malls stacked on shopping malls, and restaurant chains on every corner. Consumers consuming.

Here, Limbo, saw streets devoted to that in-between area. The pleasure circuit. Anything seedy enough that you couldn't get it in the malls, but not illegal in any major law enforcement jurisdiction. Sex stuff. Sex deviancy stuff. The softer drugs that didn't net you a corporate warrant, but were still addictive: amps, sparklers, and the like. The hardcore drug-sims. Real-D experiences like he'd been having, but instead of inhabiting the sensory memory of some lucky male porn star, the consumer would inhabit the sensory memory of some heroin junky shooting up in a dirty motel, or some kid on a heavy-duty combat stim, sprinting through back alleys and punching stop signs or hobos.

When Gash stepped out of the rain, it was into a pawn-and-gun. The pink neon side read "Gannon's Cannons." The clerk at the desk was short, burley, and sported a beard that, though it vanished behind the counter, might well have touched the floor. Time had speckled it with grey, but Gash found it impossible to tell in the shop's dim lighting how old the man was. His eyes glittered with what might have been youth, or might have been madness.

"You Gannon?"

The man nodded.

"Good, I need a cannon."

Gannon spread his arms wide, inviting Gash to approach and browse. For a pawn-and-gun, it didn't have much pawn. There was a small watch display in one corner, and a few antiques gathering dust at the far side of the shop. The vending machines on the wall by the door, unlike at the Real-D Parlour, were moderately well stocked – beer, smokes, and recreational pharmaceuticals. These were the legal ones, a bit pricier, a bit more benign, way more addictive than their street counterparts. The rest of the space had been filled to the brim with firearms.

Gash approached the clerk. "Here," he said, placing his cred-drive firmly on the counter. "I need stopping power and portability. Tell me what I can afford."

Gannon took the drive and slotted it in. Looked at it a moment, and then up at Gash, and grinned. When he spoke, it was a low baritone. "You got nothing, amigo. Nada. You can't afford the oxygen you're breathing here in my shop, let alone one of my cannons."

Gannon flipped the drive casually into the air, and Gash caught it, pocketed it. "Right," he grumbled. "Fuckin' Real-D Parlours around here are a rip."

Gannon nodded, looking down at whatever magazine he'd been looking at before Gash entered the shop.

Gash surveyed the collection of guns. There were quite a few, and a good variety to boot. Gauss weapons occupied one case, the latest in projectile death-dealing. These used magnetic propulsion to fire small metal flechettes at extreme velocities that could punch through most walls and the thickest of armor. Out of his price range for sure.

Next over were the beam weapons. These tended to be short range, flashy things. Could definitely fry a hole in someone's chest, as long as they weren't more than twenty feet away. Expensive AND inefficient.

From there, the cases seemed to be ordered chronologically through older gunpowder weapons. Sixty years of variations on the same scientific principles. Explosion propels bullet into bad guy. But what caught Gash's eye was the case of old revolvers. He'd had one like this in Seattle, before. An old .38 revolver, small and portable. It was loud and it kicked like hell, but it got the job done when it needed to. He missed it, like all of his old life as a private investigator. Never mind how he'd hated that life; now that it had been ripped away, he longed to have it back. There were a couple of these in this case, and then another one, much larger, with a longer barrel. A .44 magnum, if his memory served. Talk about a cannon.

"How much for this one?" Gash asked.

Gannon looked up just long enough to roll his eyes and say "more than free."

"Hey," Gash said, snapping his fingers. "I asked how much."

"If you had any credits, I would say 450."

Gash nodded. A fair price for an older gun like that. He removed a package from his jacket pocket, and slid it down the counter towards Gannon. Gannon caught it.

"Should be worth more like 1000," Gash said. "But I don't want to do the distribution, so give me the gun, a box of bullets, and maybe 100 on my drive, and we'll call it even."

Gannon opened it up. Inside were racks of plastic eye-droppers, each containing a couple drops worth of clear liquid. Sparklers. A short-term hallucinogenic applied directly to the eyes. Fairly harmless as street drugs went. Gash had taken it off the unconscious body of some raver/dealer who'd evidently seen Gash alone in an alley near downtown and decided to branch out into mugging. He had the kid's switchblade in his other pocket.

Gannon pulled a smallish electronic box – about the size of a small microscope – from beneath the counter, and set it down beside the eye-droppers. He pressed a few buttons, and a long thin arm extruded from the side. He dropped a single bead of liquid onto the surface of the arm's one long finger. Immediately the apparatus retracted. It buzzed and hummed for a moment, and then a pleasantly inflected robotic female voice identified the substance for all listeners as a mild hallucinogenic with no name except for the street name. Sparklers. Known for creating vivid light shows by interacting with the cones inside the eye. Street value 15-20 credits per dose. The racks added up to 100 doses, Gash had checked already.

Gannon nodded. "Not really a drug dealer here," he started.

"Can it," Gash said. "I knew half a dozen guys like you back in Seattle. You're a dealer, it doesn't matter what. And you didn't invest however many credits in that chem reader to not deal in the stuff. I don't have time to barter today, or I would have led higher."

The bearded man grinned broadly. "Okay, okay, you're some kind of street tough, sure. Fine, I know a guy who can move these and your price is fair. You have a deal."

Gannon took the package into the back, put it in a safe. Six-digit passcode, very formidable looking. When he returned, he slotted Gash's credit-drive, punched it in for 100 credits, and returned it. Grabbed the magnum, placed it on the counter. Beside it, a box of .44 cartridges. The box itself was old and faded, red with yellow wording on it. Most were worn away by the passage of time, but Gash could still see the dual 4's, and the letters "M-A-G" in bold white.

"I'll even throw the shoulder holster in," Gannon started, grabbing an old leather strap from beneath the case and offering it to Gash, "for ten credits."

Gash laughed at Gannon. "I'll trade you," he said, pulling the kid's switchblade out of his pocket.

Gannon eyed it, and nodded.

Gash put the holster on, and loaded the gun into it. Pocketed the bullets in his jacket beside the soggy smokes. "A pleasure," he said, stepping back into the night, reassured immensely by the heavy weight of the old piece against his chest, as dry as anything he owned could be, beset by the monsoon.

The rain poured and the city loomed out of the dark, but Gash felt some measure of relief. He'd set out to get himself off and get himself a gun, before that corporate assassin caught up with him. One out of two wasn't bad.

SELINA

First thing Selina noticed when she slipped the door of her tiny apartment shut behind her was that she had a new email, high priority. She keyed the security code into the terminal on the wall beside the door, and the maglocks slid into place. Flipped the two manual deadbolts into place as well. The industrial polymer of it didn't feel like much, but it'd take a bazooka to crack.

Her place was dingy, and she felt her customary twang of guilt at the pizza boxes stacked semi-neatly in the corner, the blinds drawn and thick layers of dust gathering on all of the unused kitchen surfaces. But not enough guilt to do something about it. She had shit to do. She was hot on the trail, and if she wasn't mistaken, that email blinking away at her from her custom rig was the final piece of the puzzle.

But first things first. She dropped her synth-leather duster in a puddle of water on the floor, and pulled off her soaking shirt. Monsoon rains had whipped up out of nowhere in seconds, like they always did – not that she ever got used to it. Deep blood stains had easily survived the weather – she would let it dry and work on it, but the shirt was probably ruined. Lucky her duster was black, wouldn't show the blood. Mauricio's blood. She didn't really have any fondness for the poor bastard, but he was a fixture on the streets. He was her go-to guy for paydays, and not just her. The vacuum his death produced would only be filled with blood, and it would take time. She hoped this was her final missing piece, because now was the perfect time to take an extended leave of absence from her little piece of Jacksonville. Especially if the chop shop that scooped up his body for parts had any ties to WalCo.

She stripped off the rest of her soaking clothes, tossed them into the dryer, and put on something clean. Comfortable, she slid into the soft tempur-synth-leather of her chair. Motion sensors noted her presence and a cheap gene-scan whirred for two seconds. Having verified that she was herself, the rig unlocked. She slid the cable out of the tower, and plugged it into the jack just behind her left ear. The bizarre sensation of tiny wires linking into other tiny wires that had been installed along the exterior of her cerebral cortex, and with a rush of false motion, she was inside the OS of her rig.

Selina had skinned her OS to resemble a starscape. Billions of stars everywhere you looked, galaxies and supernovae. A number of planets revolved around the gravity of her, and when she focused on them, they resolved into small icons. She pinpointed the email planet, and dove into it.

The UI for email, jacked in, was much like standard email UI for the last hundred or so years. White background with black text. Some would consider it gratuitous to jack in just for email, but Selina lived for the rush of diving into cyberspace. She could've chosen to assign a voice to read her email to her, but it went faster this way.

She called up the high priority message, and scanned it quickly. Sure enough, her application for admission into Deep Earth had been accepted! She now possessed login access to thousands of scans from the latest and greatest in satellite tech, the Deep Earth Quantum Tunneler.

Her heart pounding, she pre-paid her membership for the first year using some of the funds from the cred-drive she'd taken off Mauricio. She hammered out a very brief thank you note to Hemmingway for the false credentials she'd commissioned in order to gain membership to archaeology's most exclusive provider of satellite imagery. And then she was in, floating above the Earth from afar. From outer space, between the cracks in the thick cloud layer, you could still see some green on the planet's surface; though the predominant colors were different shades of brown, and of course the deep blue of the ocean. From afar, an enormous white storm system beginning to spin deep in the Pacific looked more majestic than terrifying.

Bright orange pins – hundreds of them – protruded from the digitally rendered globe. Each of these represented a point of potential interest, something beneath the planet's surface that registered to the Deep Earth software as manmade. Something that had been cross-referenced with known features of modern infrastructure and found to have no known correlation.

She reached out and spun the world until she was floating in the stratosphere above the Mediterranean, descending towards Turkey or, to be more exact, Rhodes. There was an orange pin there, and her heart soared. She knew it. For years she'd been ridiculed in archaeology chatrooms and on discussion boards for her theory. She'd even been denied admission to the Florida State University Department of Classics, back when she thought she could somehow manage to earn those credentials rather than fake them. But here it was, the DEQT had found something. She grabbed for it, and then she was hovering over a satellite image of the island of Rhodes, watching Deep Earth render what it had found.

Her moment was nigh. As a child, Selina had received a precious gift from her father. The man worked three odd jobs, but had always dreamed of uncovering ancient secrets in archaeological digs. They'd watched and re-watched old Indiana Jones and Tomb Raider movies together. When he realized Selina had grown to share that interest on her tenth birthday, he gave her a small journal, the notes of a mid-21st century French archaeologist named Rembert. Selina had quickly learned French – a feat her father had never managed to find time for – and plumbed the depths of the little old journal. Rembert was chasing rumors that pieces of the Colossus – one of the Seven Wonders of the ancient world – had not been melted down by the Ottomans in the 7th century A.D., as was commonly thought to be the case. If the notes were to be believed (and Selina did believe them, then and forever), Rembert managed to find a foot, whole and intact. He mentioned that from his analysis, it did not appear that the Colossus fell over during an earthquake. There were signs of melting, as though intense heat had caused the fall of the great wonder.

His notes became increasingly paranoid from here. He talked of a secret war that caused the destruction of the Colossus and the subsequent damage to the city of Rhodes that was attributed to an earthquake. Even later, the notes began to reference the Knights Hospitaller, the Catholic Military order that eventually gave way to the Knights of Rhodes, who eventually became the Sovereign Military Order of Malta, an independent organization that, in modern times, offered aid to victims of natural disasters and plagues. Rembert believed they were chasing him.

Selina wasn't sure how much she believed. The Knights Hospitaller would not be formed for more than a thousand years after the fall of the Colossus, so that seemed like utter paranoia. But perhaps they took possession of the foot when they occupied the island in the early 14th century? Rembert did not ever make clear where he'd found the intact piece of the great wonder, and modern histories made no mention of Rembert or his supposed discoveries. Was there a secret war in Rhodes in the 220s B.C.? Selina didn't know. But she knew something wasn't right with the commonly believed story of the Colossus. A small independent merchant city builds the largest statue in the ancient world, only to have it toppled by an earthquake that created no tsunami? That went unnoticed on surrounding cities and islands? It didn't add up.

And now, finally, Deep Earth had dredged up some answers for her. What would she find? Burial sites throughout the island, dead Rhodian soldiers consumed in some ancient civil war? Something beneath the earth where the Colossus had once stood, some kind of sabotage that had caused the disaster? A discovery like this would surely get Selina a University job. It was her way out. Legitimacy in the field, freedom from the hard-scrabble street life she'd cobbled together out of the death of her parents a decade ago. And then she could finally pursue her true dream, exploring the roots of her family tree in ancient Mayan civilization.

DEQT produced unprecedented imagery, and thousands of gigs of data were being loaded into her map simulation. When it finally loaded, all she could do was stare, dumbfounded. There was no burial site, nothing that could have been dug by man. What she saw was a hole, perfectly cylindrical. Fully rendered by Deep Earth, it began about a kilometer beneath the lowlands of Rhodes, just east of some steep mountain. Fifty meters in diameter exactly, it descended past the limits of even the DEQT. There was no way.

She reached out and made a motion as though she were pulling a rope towards herself. All of the data on this pin came whooshing towards her in a torrent. There were pages of analyses of soil content and rock types. There were a few comments from others in her field. These were nearly identical, lamenting that Deep Earth wasn't doing a good enough job at filtering out natural phenomena, and that they should sell data to geologists instead of archaeologists. And indeed, though it looked nothing like any natural event that Selina had ever heard of, her first impulse was that this was a false alarm. Some kind of unknown natural event must have caused this. Nothing manmade could have caused such a pit. That many kilometers of solid rock? The cost to dig that wide and that deep even with modern technology would be prohibitive, there was no way it had anything to do with her secret war, with the fall of the Colossus.

And yet. Her gut told her brain that it was wrong. That it dismissed too readily what it didn't understand. She *knew* something wasn't right with the modern conception of Rhodian history. And sure enough she had found something inexplicable. It wasn't the loose thread she'd expected to find, but it was the only thread available. She must pull it, she knew, and see what unraveled.

For that, she would need money. Much more than she'd gotten off Mauricio. She archived all of the data on the Pit of Rhodes, as she privately dubbed it, and returned to her starscape OS. Checked in on a few things. All of her fake credentials were still in order, undisturbed. Undiscovered. In about two hours, half a dozen universities in the Florida area would receive a proposal from a distinguished academic with graduate degrees in classics and anthropology. A woman named Selina Kan. That proposal would seek to investigate the connection between a recently discovered natural hole in the deep portions of the crust and a number of Rhodian folk legends.

It was the sort of unglamorous proposal that would appeal to the least imaginative in the field. It should be a good fit for funding. Not big money, but enough. At least one of the schools would bite. They had to. This thing, this pit – it was her ticket out of this life. That she didn't know exactly what she would find didn't matter, because she knew she'd find something.

GASH

As far as Gash was concerned, The Supreme held the record for the shittiest place he'd ever spent a night. The carpeting, a hideous coloration somewhere between vomit and phlegm, torn at nearly every corner to reveal a slick and moldy tile floor beneath, vied with the dim and permanently flickering neon lighting for the lobby's best feature. Drifters buying what the desk clerks were selling accrued each night in the corners and on the ancient lobby furniture, mauve in places that were not stained with something else, ripped and broken in more sections than not. The stench of sweat and bodily fluids followed close behind.

The desk clerks seemed to rotate daily, no one clerk ever repeating, but each a near-perfect replication of the last. White guys with soggy dreadlocks; baggy, half-torn clothing; and a permanent, sagging grin. Today's clerk leered emptily past him, making little movements with his mouth, obviously tripping on something much heavier than sparklers.

Gash had prepaid for ten days. Though he found himself coming up on his eighth day, he suspected that at the eleventh day, nobody would notice if he just held onto his old-style metal key. There didn't seem to be much book-keeping going on back there behind the counter. It didn't take a private detective to determine that the place was a front for some low-level gang to run drugs out of. Probably stayed out of the line of fire of any corporate sec teams by doubling as a place for mid-level execs to bring their slum hookers for a night of hot fun. He shook his head. Why anyone would roll the STD dice with some ragged street-girl when they could bang a porn star through the magic of a Real-D rig was beyond him.

He stepped gingerly past a gaggle of four or five drifters that had sprawled almost entirely in front of the elevator, almost slipping on a slick patch of exposed tiling, wet with something best left unidentified. And then the elevator doors were closing behind him, and he was on his way up to the third floor.

Dark thoughts swirled within, and he grimaced. But at least they kept his mind off the elevator, rattling violently; crawling painfully up towards the second floor.

Someone was on to him. Yesterday, he'd been made. A young woman on the street, paying him just a little too much attention, and then suddenly turning away, her personal computer in her hand, the PCom holodisplay showing what looked like maybe a face. Like maybe his.

There was definitely a contract on his head. WalCo did not take kindly at all to the sort of stunt he'd pulled back in Seattle, and they would be coming for him. He'd chosen Jacksonville simply for geography: the Florida sprawl was the farthest metro from Seattle, and he found himself stuck here until he could make contact with someone who could create him some convincing documents. Any corporation with the authority to issue passports would immediately flag Nagash Jensen (his hated real name, the product of idiot parents and their ironic hipster love for 20th century Norwegian death metal) and see that WalCo had a warrant out for his death. He needed out of the country, and he needed a fake identity to manage it.

And now he'd been made, and a WalCo contractor was surely

tracking him. Buying the cam footage outside any building he might've walked by, interrogating strangers who would be too afraid to lie, showing pictures of him, wanted outlaw Nagash Jensen.

He adjusted the shoulder holster, the weight of the gun his only reassurance. A hired assassin got the jump on him, and that would be it, gun or no gun. But he was on red alert, and he knew what to look for.

The elevator ground to a halt on the third floor, the old steel doors screeching slowly open and settling into place with a deep metallic groan. The whole car shuddered once. Gash stepped out. Still better than what was in the stairways, he reminded himself.

A tall girl in mismatched stiletto heels patrolled the third floor hallway. Her skin was somewhere between olive and cappuccino; he found it difficult to tell beneath the layer of grime. Long brown hair fell tangled from her scalp down to the small of her back. Her synth-leather one piece had seen better days, but the faux-fur jacket that draped her thin shoulders seemed new enough: Business must've still been coming her way. Beneath the shabby exterior, Gash thought, she had quite the body. Nothing, of course, like the Real-D girl he'd been with earlier that night. Or not been with, per se, but rather had experienced non-vicariously, as the ads would have put it. Still, she was good to look at.

When she saw him she made a bee-line for him. There was something hard in her eyes, and he tensed. Was she really a hooker panhandling for business in the halls of The Supreme? Or was she the assassin, found him already, a thin pistol in her tiny clutch bag, or a knife in her boot?

"Hey love," she said, affecting a British accent. "Need some company tonight?"

He groaned inwardly at the horrid attempt to conceal her Deep South roots, but relaxed too. This was no assassin, this was just a down-on-her-luck girl from the half-drowned back-country swamps of Florida making a go of it in the big metro sprawl.

"No," he grunted, brushing past her.

"I'll show you a real good time, gov'nor," she said.

"Sweet hell, woman," he turned slowly. "That accent's not fooling a soul. Not even the dullest asshole in this shitpile would believe you were from anywhere but the Florida boonies."

"Well," she said, the accent gone like that. "Fuck you too."

As she turned to go, he called to her. "Wait," he said.

She spun around.

"How much?" He didn't know what'd gotten into him. Maybe it was serotonin flooding his system after he realized she wasn't the assassin. Maybe it was the proximity to death that had him yearning for a woman's touch. Or maybe he was just still horny from being cut off at the Real-D Parlour. But if she proved cheaper than the Real-D experience, then he could potentially still go two for two on his plan for the day.

"You kidding me, asshole?" she said.

"How much," he growled again.

She seemed to consider him for a moment. Numbers and values racing back and forth in her head, the calculus of business. "One-eighty for the night," she said. "Thirty credit asshole fee on top of my usual rate."

"I've only got 100," he said, eyes locked on hers. They were deep brown, wide and unblinking.

She held eye contact until Gash looked away. Then she shrugged her shoulders. "Fuck it," she said.

And then they were in his tiny cell, a makeshift wall splitting what once was a much larger hotel room in half. A tiny mattress sagged with age atop on an ancient wooden bedframe, broken in a dozen places and supported by a ramshackle assortment of duct tape and braces made from moldy wood. He was lucky to have a small bathroom, sink and toilet and unbroken mirror, the plumbing occasionally working if he was having a good day.

The hooker began stripping down before he'd closed the door, and he followed suit, awkwardly. Gash had not been with a woman – a real woman – since Serena. Serena, who had ODed the day after she told him she was going out for an addiction remover, that she knew a third party selling them with no strings attached: no corporate indenturement, no religious conversion required. When he'd gotten home that night, to their home, there she'd been on the floor.

There was something in his eyes and the girl was staring at him. He finished undressing quickly, the memory shoved deep in a corner, the whatever in his eyes blinked away until his vision cleared again. Closer, with her clothes off and in the somewhat brighter light of his room, Gash realized she couldn't have been more than her early twenties. Too young for him by his reckoning, but that didn't matter now that he found himself staring at her slender body, perky breasts, the right much larger than the left.

She stood there waiting for him, not impatient or frightened, but bored, uncomfortable with the extended silence. He looked hard, followed the curves of her down her smooth legs to her toes, and back up again. This felt all kinds of wrong, and he set that aside too, along with everything he'd been thinking about rolling the dice no more than five minutes ago. He wanted her, and this wouldn't be the worst choice he made this month, not by a longshot. He wrapped his arms around her, and she relaxed into him, relieved he supposed, that things were finally back on their normally scheduled course.

SAGE MENOTTI

"Sage."

The voice seemed to arise from the depths of an endless black cavern. But then, Sage came gradually to realize that everything was black.

"Sage." They recognized the voice. Hiroyuki, Sage's partner, that's who the voice belonged to. A baritone Japanese voice enunciating French words from far, far away. "Sage, are you okay?"

Sage opened their eyes. The deep bright sun, screened though it was by the Parisian smog, felt impossibly bright. Sage's head throbbed.

"What happened?" The words poured like gravel in Sage's mouth.

"Gerard got the jump on you, clocked you from behind," Hiroyuki said. "I thought you might be dead, at first."

Gerard. That name meant something. But what? There was too much cotton lining Sage's brain, a layer of clouds that blocked one part of the brain from the next, obstructing the synapses from making basic connections. Hiroyuki said they had been hit over the head. Must be to do with that. But who was Gerard?

"Look, an android!" came a voice, young and male, from the periphery.

Sage felt a white-hot anger, something well-defined. The anger blasted away the cotton, a solar wind cleansing the poison atmosphere from the planet of Sage's brain.

"Android?" Sage said, voice calm, rising from the pavement.

"Oh shit," Hiroyuki said, shaking his head.

"Yeah," the kid said, stepping forward. "Android, you heard me." His hair had been spiked solid and wrapped in barbed wire. He wore a long black synth-leather overcoat, even though it must've been over 33 degrees. Sage wondered how he slept with hair like that.

"I used to be like you," Sage said. "But I found I was always thinking with my bits instead of my brain, and getting into all kinds of trouble. You should consider having the surgery done."

The French punk opened his mouth to respond, but Sage lashed out, grabbing him by the face, their fingers sinking into the soft flesh between upper and lower jaw. He clawed at their arm, but Sage was far too strong. For all his bravado, the punk was a weakling.

"Listen, this has been fun," Sage said. "But you're obstructing an Interpol investigation and if you don't get the hell out of here right now, things are going to get much worse for you."

They released their grip on the kid's face, and without a further word, he spun and ran from the two Interpol agents.

Hiroyuki laughed. "I still don't understand where they get this slur from, 'android.'"

Sage sighed. "From the English language originally, 'androgynous' was benignly misused to describe folks like me who had gone through sex removal surgery. This was benignly shortened to 'andro,' which was then extended to 'android,' implying that we since we don't have sex organs, we might as well be robots."

Hiroyuki finally rose from kneeling, dusting off his own tan slacks, readjusting his tie. He smiled at them. "It doesn't seem like an insult to me. Life-like robots are the cutting edge of technology right now. But I suppose it's all in the intent of the person using the word, no?"

Sage looked at Hiroyuki. What a strange man. His diminutive presence belied a moderately above-average build. Gentle eyes cloaked a predatory intelligence that he had already put to great use in the investigation. He dressed conservatively, though each tie the man owned seemed to feature the Buddha in some capacity (in this case the red tie was scattered with tiny likenesses, like small yellow dots). Hiroyuki had not been their partner for long, and they had not gotten him figured out just yet, not by a longshot. Regardless, this line of conversation tread on dangerous ground. Sage had already lost two partners on account of their sex. Or lack thereof.

"Look, Hiro, let's not get into it. We have a dangerous criminal on the loose."

Hiroyuki's eyes seemed to shrug. "If you had not run off without me, the chase might already be over."

"True," Sage said. "I apologize. Been having some issues with partners lately."

"Well now is the time to set those aside and fill me in. You've been chasing this Gerard for a very long time, but have shared very little. Do you have anything?"

Sage considered for a moment. They did have something, now that he mentioned it. "Last time Gerard popped up in Paris, an informant of mine put me onto a safehouse owned by his organization. I staked it out for a week, but he never showed. Perhaps now that he knows we're on to him, he'll make an appearance there. In fact, now that I'm saying the words, I'm almost sure of it. He'll try to go to ground before he flees the country."

Hiroyuki laughed. "His organization? All I really know, coming on this late, is that Gerard's wanted for several murders around the Mediterranean. What organization?"

Sage opened their mouth to fill their new partner in, but then thought better of it. Nobody heard the full story and thought anything but "conspiracy theory." After all, the Knights Hospitaller, reinvented as the Knights of Malta many hundreds of years ago, sounded more like the villainous organization in one of those old conspiracy books from the early 21st century, not like a real-life body condoning and sheltering murderers in an underground shadow war playing out across the continent.

"I'll fill you in later," Sage said, hoisting their gear bag off the street from where it had fallen. "Let's go get him first."

"Lead the way, partner," Hiroyuki replied, and Sage did, plunging into the crowd.

GASH

Fortunately, among Gash's many conditions and problems, insomnia stood at the forefront. Three hours after his lady of the night had passed out in the bed beside him, he continued to stare at the ceiling, waiting impatiently for sleep's arrival. Waiting for an end to the tumultuous battle between the happy part of his brain, basking in serotonin; and the moralizing part of his brain, upset at his choices and how they might affect him or this too-young woman.

So when there came a scraping at the door, almost imperceptible, it did not go unperceived. Gash slid out of bed, grabbing the hand cannon from on top of the small Port-o-Bible that came standard in the bedside drawer of each hotel bedroom in the U.S.

The girl, who'd identified herself as Lulu, woke slowly, her eyes going wide as she took him in. She opened her mouth, but he silenced her with a cupped hand. Leaned in and whispered to her before she could get the wrong notion and begin to struggle. "Listen," he said. And she did. He removed his hand when he was sure she heard the lockpicks scraping in the old metal lock.

It was taking the would-be assassin an awfully long time to get the door opened. Probably wasn't used to mechanical locks, probably would've already been in the room and dancing on Gash's corpse if it had been a standard digital lock.

He rose to his feet, naked except for the magnum in both hands. Lulu watched from the bed, utterly still. A thought struck him, and he leaned towards her. "Hide under the bed," he said. "Just in case. If he kills me he'll kill you, unless he doesn't know you're in here."

She opened her mouth to protest, but he cut her off. "Just do it, I don't want one more death on my conscience."

She rolled off the bed and slid under. He positioned himself just around the corner from the door, and waited. Finally, a click. The lock opened, and the assassin slipped into the room, utterly silent, the soft click of the door shutting the only sound he or she made.

That was Gash's cue. He spun around the corner and fired two blasts from the hand cannon. It roared, deafening, and kicked hard in his hands. He felt as though his arms were on the verge of coming off at the elbows, his eardrums exploding. But the black-clad assassin dropped hard to the floor and did not move.

Gash flipped the lights on and had a closer look. The two slugs had punched through a thick Kevlar body suit, but not come back out the other side. This was heavy duty armor – good thing he'd had a heavy duty revolver.

The hired killer came fully wared. When Gash looked him over he found a high-end neural jack installed behind the right ear, could see in his dead eyes a faint red tint – sub-ocular infra-lenses, very high tech – and last of all, thin razors (presumably retractable) protruding from beneath each fingernail of his right hand.

This was real top-of-the-line stuff. WalCo had pulled out all the stops on this one. The good news, though, was that the gear alone would be worth thousands. Suppressed high-velocity automatic gauss pistol, a suite of hacking tools in a pouch on his back, a brand new piece of tech in the form of a modular grappling tool that could double as a harpoon gun. Gannon would wet himself over all of this.

"Jesus," Lulu said from behind him. "Someone must want you bad. What'd you do?"

"Trust me when I tell you that you don't want to know. We'll just say that WalCo's pissed about it, and leave it at that."

"WalCo? Damn, boy, you are fucked. Best get out of the country."

"If I could find someone in this god-forsaken town who could make me something that would fool AirCorp's battery of security tests, I'd already be on a plane," he growled.

When she said nothing for a moment, he turned. She bit her lower lip and looked away.

"Holy Jesus, you know someone," Gash said.

She nodded. "And he won't like me connecting him to a stranger – especially a stranger with this much heat on him – but you thought of me. Even with your life on the line, you thought of me. I," she stopped.

"I get it," Gash said. "And when we pawn this hitman's gear, I'll make sure you get a cut. A finder's fee."

Later, when they'd piled the gear on the bed, Gash stood at the room's lone window. Through the decades of accumulated filth ingrained within the panes, he watched the narrow strip of city visible from the third floor. Halogen streetlamps lit the torrents of rain that continued to pour from the sky, flooding into the gutters and pushing trash along the sidewalk. Dark forms moved beneath the weight of all that water, people going about private business in the middle of the night, the nightlife undiminished by the perpetual monsoon. In the distance, Gash could see the new part of the sprawl, the hyper-towers. Cloud scrapers. Thousands of stories high, they skewered rainclouds and shone brightly down at the older, dirtier portions of the city. Beacons for the wealthy, and for the would-be success stories scrounging at the outskirts for a slim hope of a good future in the corporate womb of some mega-entity like WalCo. He clenched his fists.

Somewhere in this mess, Lulu knew a guy. In a few hours, they'd be out in it again, and they'd go to Lulu's guy. Gash would have papers, a fake identity good enough to get him out of the country. Would WalCo follow? Maybe. Maybe not. But if they didn't follow, he vowed, he would start a new life in a new country. Find a new Serena, a peaceful job that made him no enemies, and live a quiet life.

Gash turned away from the window. First, though, there was a body to drag to a nearby chop shop, gear to pawn over at Gannon's, a guy to see about a passport, and a ticket out of town with his name on it.

GASH

By the time Gash stood at the door outside of Lulu's fixer's condo building, the sun had already begun to set. A rare thing, to see the sun in monsoon season, but there it was, shining down orange through the thick haze of atmosphere and smog and humidity. He sweat buckets in the heat of it, so it might as well have been raining. Impossible to escape the thick sheen of moisture that had coated him from the first hour he set foot in this god-forsaken hellhole.

But soon he'd be on his way out. They'd gotten a small fortune from cannibalizing the WalCo contractor's wares at the body shop, and selling his gear at Gannon's. A rip-off if you thought about how much that stuff cost on the open market, but factoring in the sort of heat that all parties knew would be associated with every proprietary piece of cyberware and hardware, about what Gash had expected. A piece of that would go to Lulu, and the rest probably to her guy for fake papers. The tech for detecting forgeries had come so far that good forgeries were an upper echelon piece of work for a skilled operator. Definitely not cheap.

The building seemed to shimmer in the bright haze of the day.

Her guy lived in one of the newer condo buildings that had gone up between the work-town part of the city and Limbo. Close enough to the corporate holdings to benefit from the security presence of their crime patrols, but close enough to work the streets in some of the gray areas that a corporation would frown upon. These were people with money and enough corp connections to stay outside of indenturement, but who didn't work for any publicly traded entities. Lulu knew a guy with clout.

Gash followed her into the lobby. The front desk concierge-guard looked up from the desk, but didn't move. They were out of place here. Faux-wood paneling in a rich mahogany, as good as the real stuff as far as Gash could make out. Tinted windows, luxurious synth-leather recliners in tightly knit seating arrangements that had clearly almost never been used. The guard seemed unperturbed. Probably, Gash figured, he had a battery of automated turrets queued up at the click of a button. Place like this had to have something like that.

"Hey, Lulu," he said from behind the desk. "Here on business?"

"Not the usual kind," she said. "Hemmingway's..." she hesitated and looked at Gash. "He's not expecting me."

The security guard looked at Gash and then back at Lulu. "Got it. I'll page him for you." His mouth kept moving after this, but no more sound emerged. After a moment Gash realized it was sub-vocalization. This desk guard had some high tech wares of his own. If there had been any doubt about the security, this removed it. Turrets, a fast response team hidden away in the next room, something. Best not to act up. Best to stay on this Hemmingway's good side.

Lulu and Gash stood side by side, awkward in the silence of the waiting. What would Hemmingway say? What was he like? Some tech geek no doubt, but if he lived here he had connections, and no way would Gash risk pushing him around. There wouldn't be a lot of options if the price was too high. He looked at Lulu. She met his gaze for a second and then looked down at her feet.

"Don't take this the wrong way, but if you're working places like this, what were you doing at the Supreme last night?"

Lulu looked him directly in the eyes, and held it there for a long time before she answered. "This isn't my normal place of business. But sometimes wealthy people like to call out for someone from a different part of town. Hemmingway says he likes me because I'm 'real,' and with what he pays I don't ask questions when he calls. If he called more often, maybe I wouldn't have to..." she trailed off, looking away.

Gash checked his PCom. It had been ten minutes since the desk guard paged this Hemmingway. What was going on? Gash was getting antsy. "Hey, man," Gash started.

The guard cut him off with a sour look, and Lulu grabbed Gash's shoulder. "Don't," she said. "Just wait."

Eventually the desk guard perked up – message incoming, no doubt – and then waved the two of them forward. "Hemmingway will see you now," he said. "You know the way, right Lulu?"

Lulu flashed the guy a thumbs up and then they were on the elevator, Lulu said "Fifteen" and the doors slid effortlessly shut. No cranking deathtrap like the one at the Supreme, this. The car cruised smoothly and silently upwards, a soft, pleasant classical melody playing from the speakers. The walls, fully digital, displayed an ad for a travel agency selling week-long packages for visits to Lunar-City, the first arcology on the Moon. Instead of an elevator, they stood on a black-sand beach carefully hand-crafted inside the domed bubble that provided Lunar-City with all of its oxygen, and protected it from the vastness of space.

"Leap like Superman, swim like Aquaman. Lounge in luxury on the black-sand beaches of Lunar-City. Apply today for extra-planetary visas for you and your family!"

The ad voice took a deep breath, winding up for another pitch, when the elevator dinged and the doors opened, the blackness of space parting to reveal more mahogany paneling and plush maroon carpeting. Out they stepped, and Lulu led Gash down the halls. An older couple passed them, eying Gash suspiciously, looking past Lulu carefully.

They came to a stop before a door. Like all the others they'd passed, this seemed a door like any other. Painted a complimentary mahogany tone, so as to fit nicely in with the hall's décor, it didn't seem to be a particularly foreboding door. But Gash could see Lulu's hand shaking as she knocked on it twice, and then stepped back, eyes straight forward, waiting.

It swung open to reveal a man whose most striking feature could be nothing other than his size. His considerable girth filled the doorway. A tangle of black hair rested atop a deeply bronze-colored face. Small eyes peered out from beneath the mop, looking from Lulu to Gash and back again. He wore only a t-shirt and gym shorts, the print on the front of the enormous shirt apparently some kind of public service message about the value of reading books. Gash tried not to stare.

Evidently he did a poor job. "What, you've never seen a Samoan before?"

Gash had not, though he was familiar. He said nothing, preferring to let Lulu navigate the introductions. He had a notion that what Lulu did for Hemmingway made her the perfect person to introduce him.

"Hemmingway," Lulu said. "This is Gash. He's a good guy – with money – and he needs your help. I hope it's okay..." she trailed off.

"With money," Hemmingway imitated. "Why does everyone think money's all I care about?" Before Lulu could answer, Hemmingway cut her off. "No, don't worry, it's okay. Come on in with all your money, Gash," he said, stepping back from the door and inviting them inside with a wave.

Gash followed Lulu and the big Samoan inside. His breath caught in his throat at the luxury of the place. Floor-to-ceiling windows gave a staggering view of the Jacksonville skyline. Sleek black furniture faced a wall-sized holovision screen that probably cost more than Gash had made in a year as a P.I. in Seattle. A bar lined the far side of the room, stacked with bottles. Two small refrigerators were inset beneath.

Hemmingway gestured at these. "Lulu, help yourself to a Bloody Mary, or anything else you want. Gash, step into my office, and let's talk about what we can do for each other."

Gash followed Hemmingway through another door, and found himself in a rather spartan room. There were two desks – one empty, one with a great big HV projector on it. Four large quantum PC towers had been mounted in a rack on the upper part of the far wall, and this all fed into a rig in the center of the room, protected by an alloy mesh plating. Cords blossomed from the rig in each direction. The walls seemed at first glance to be painted a plain white, and there were no windows.

When the door slid shut behind Gash, Hemmingway turned to him. There were two chairs, one at each desk. Hemmingway pulled them both free so that he and Gash could sit facing each other.

Gash slid comfortably into the luxurious tempur-material that made up the cushions for the Hemmingway-sized chair. It was wonderful. He'd happily have slept in that chair for days. But any thought of relaxation vanished when – like the elevator – the entire wall-space of the room switched on and began to display digital images. Images of Gash. He did not move, not one inch. He only watched – watched himself shooting his way out of a WalCo facility.

"You've got a lot of heat on you," Hemmingway said.

Gash said nothing.

"This is all I could find on why, which I find bizarre, because I can find anything that's out there. I can find what you ate for breakfast ten years ago if you paid with a cred-drive. I can hack WalCo's security files in my sleep, and it took me less than ten minutes to find this after I saw your face in the lobby. So I know WalCo's after you and I assume that means Lulu brought you to me for a way out of the country. But I want to know *why*. *Why* is WalCo after you, and *why* are you on film shooting your way out of a WalCo research facility and *why* are you not dead yet?"

The pulse of Gash's blood roared in his temples. Fight or flight kicked in with a vengeance, and he wanted badly to choose flight. But that was the whole point, wasn't it? He couldn't flee the country without this Samoan, who was apparently also a gifted hacker. So he remained in his chair, every muscle and fiber of his body straining to flee.

On the screen, he ducked and rolled out of a doorway and came up firing, taking out two security guards with a .38 revolver. A third came around the corner behind him and tried to put him in a choke-hold – *should've just shot me*, Gash thought – and Gash twisted out of it, breaking the man's arm and then snapping his neck with a knee to the face.

"Also when you're done explaining all of this, you've got to tell me where you learned that shit," Hemmingway said, evidently excited by the action.

Gash took a deep breath and closed his eyes. It was too disconcerting, seeing himself like that. "I don't know much. I was a P.I. in Seattle and someone hired me. I knew better than to take the job – too much money, too vague. It was fishy and my gut said no, but my bank account said yes. Sometimes your bank account won't take no for an answer, I guess."

"I had days like that, back in the beginning," Hemmingway nodded.

"The job was to find a kidnapped WalCo scientist, and the client was anonymous. I followed the trail. WalCo was searching for her too, or so I thought. Eventually I realized they'd actually kidnapped her from themselves and moved her to a secret research facility. I tried to go in and extract her, but security was too tight. Barely got out with my life, and I've been running ever since. My client pulled my expense account and left me with nothing but a note, disappointed that he'd 'overestimated' me." Gash took a deep breath and opened his eyes. "You know what I know. Oh, and I learned to fight in the Army. One of the last Spec Ops teams before the military was officially disbanded."

Hemmingway rubbed the top of his head fiercely. "That's all very intense, Mr. Jensen. You're older than you look." He considered the story for a moment. "What kind of scientist?"

"She was a biochemist," Gash said. "Pharmaceuticals, officially."

"Well that's a hell of a story, but I believe all of it. If only because I have the tape from WalCo's security banks. It looks like you killed nine security guards on your way out of that research facility after you were caught."

He looked away, but everywhere his eyes settled, there was more of the video, him reloading his revolver, taking apart the WalCo sec-team. He used to get like that on missions, too. When someone came after him, a second brain took over his primary brain. Instincts. The same guts that he'd relied on as a P.I. They turned him into a monster. Nine kills getting out of WalCo – it was actually ten, but the fifth hadn't been captured on camera – and that paled in comparison to his last years in the military back in the day. He had blood on his hands, blood by the bucket. He considered them, weathered and deep-lined. Did he even deserve to escape the country? Before he could answer himself, Hemmingway spoke again.

"So here's the arrangement. A friend of mine – she would say business partner, but she's a cynic like our Lulu out there – will shortly be coming for a visit. She's going to be setting up an expedition to Rhodes, so obviously she'll need a competent bodyguard."

"Roads? Which roads?" Gash asked.

Hemmingway sighed. "I suppose it was too much to hope that the Army taught you geography. R-h-o-d-e-s," he spelled it out, "is an island just off the coast of Turkey. Former Greek territory. Basically in the fringe of the Mid-East shitstorm, and with no major corporate interests to keep the peace."

"Why the hell is your friend going there?"

Hemmingway shrugged, his chair wobbling and creaking under the weight of the gesture. "She's always fancied herself an archaeologist, and she thinks she's found something there to dig up. Some ancient secret to uncover. It doesn't matter, she got the project funded, so she's got money. She'll be coming to me shortly for muscle, and I think you fit the bill."

"I'm no bodyguard, Hemmingway," Gash said. "And I think you know it. I came to you to buy a fake passport and get myself out of the country. I want to steer as clear of conflict as I can, live out my days in some quiet corner of the world that hasn't been ruined yet. Not looking for a job today, sorry."

"But this job is your only way out. What'd you get from selling the gear on that hitman earlier today, 3000? You barely have a decent down payment on what I'm going to have to do to get you out of the country with the kind of heat you have. I mean, you killed *nine* WalCo guards, my friend. The heat I'm going to get just by proximity to you, you think you can buy all this for 3000?"

Gash rose, and took one step towards the door. Last thing in the world he wanted was to come near that hotbed of partisan religious violence and genocide. On the digital display all around him, he was about to escape. One more guard stood between him and the fire exit towards the outside world, towards the shelter of the Seattle sprawl. You couldn't tell on the camera, but the guard was a kid; she had a nose ring and a tuft of pink hair peeking out from beneath the alloy helmet. When she saw him she tried to get a bead on him with her weapon. Her gauss rifle kicked, but the shot went wide. Must've been a rookie. And he was on her then – out of ammo at this point, but that hadn't stopped him – he pulled the knife from her own boot and jammed it into her throat. After, he was out the door, the harsh sunlight flooding in and over her body, automatically kicking the camera's light sensors down a few notches, the display dimming to accommodate the change in brightness.

The things he'd done to try to find peace in this life since Serena... well, what was one more job? Protecting some archaeologist couldn't be that bad. He'd been a soldier, he'd been a P.I. He'd been a vagrant, and now he'd be a bodyguard. Maybe it would be a nice change of pace, protecting instead of attacking. He turned back from the door and sat back down.

"Let's talk details, then," Gash said.

—

Hemmingway grinned. "Let's."

SELINA

Hemmingway's avatar, a stunning replica of the 20th century author from whom he had taken his name, sat delicately across from her at the table, grinning. Selina wouldn't have known the author's face, except that Hemmingway had brought it up on at least three separate occasions, and she'd run a quick web search to confirm the likeness. "The author in his prime," Hemmingway would say. High forehead, slicked back hair, dark. Small, thin moustache, dark. Chin distinct and protruding. He wore a white button down shirt and a beige vest, khaki pants.

She found it gratuitous. Plenty of people designed custom avatars with little or nothing to do with their own likeness; typically they would mirror a celebrity, or represent a generic vision of beauty. Sometimes a monster, alien, vampire, or something equally otherworldly. She had no use for such things. Her avatar had been painstakingly designed to resemble herself. That's what an avatar was, after all. A representation of the self. Her avatar sported her long black hair, tied in a ponytail as was her way. The silver band that pierced her lower lip just off-center to the right in reality featured prominently on her avatar as well. Its face shared her narrow features – delicate, a boy had once described them, just before she'd hit him with a jab to the nose (that had been the end of *that* date).

Her main compromise to imagination was the avatar's clothing. Her avatar wore a bulky white space suit, her best attempt at a replica of what Neil Armstrong had worn when he walked on the moon over a century ago. The helmet was missing, to reveal her face of course. She'd drawn many a comment over the years for her cumbersome choice, or the occasional snide remark that her spacesuit wasn't doing her much good without a helmet. Naturally, this all lacked the remotest relevance in cyberspace, but that didn't stop the young men in the circles she frequented from being spiteful.

Hemmingway hosted their meeting on his private server. He had a number of simulations available, she knew – he was an avid gamer as well as a hacker and a "procurer of services," as he liked to refer to himself (middleman, Selina would say) – but for the meeting it was simply his digital manor house.

Painstakingly coded, the manor stood outthrust on a thin piece of rocky land. All around, the jagged coastline roared as the ocean beset it with wave upon wave. Salt spray erupted every few seconds from the churn below, and with the manor windows open, Selina could smell it as surely as if she were standing on the real ocean's edge outside the Jacksonville sprawl. Except here was more pure, mixed in with none of the diesel fumes, vomit, rotten fish, stink of sex, and other assorted accoutrements that accompanied it in reality. The sensory coding bespoke a great deal of time and money, especially considering that only a relatively small portion of Hemmingway's clientele would be wired for full neural connectivity with the web. It was gratuitous. Which didn't stop it from being damn impressive.

The home itself towered upwards, in stark defiance of the laws of gravity (of which, here, there were none that Hemmingway had not coded himself). She had seen it from the outside many times, for Hemmingway preferred to load his guests into the simulation up the

—

path a ways and walk them in. The building had something like six or seven stories to it. In reality it would probably have measured out at over 15,000 square feet, all told. It was white, Victorian in style, all spires and turrets and ornate protrusions on each floor. If you stared at it for too long, the home would seem to seethe with its own impossibility. Selina found it best not to.

She had never visited the upper stories, nor had she known anyone to do so. The meetings invariably took place in the first floor dining area, just off to the side of the kitchen. A sturdy oak table, ornate Victorian chairs that should in no way have been half as comfortable as they were programmed to be.

Hemmingway's servant entered, pouring each of them tea. Earl Grey, he had once told her. The tea was delicate, elegant. Just hot enough, with hints of what she'd once looked up online to discover was called bergamot, the oil of a French citrus fruit that had gone extinct some few decades ago. Far less elegant than the tea, Hemmingway's servant turned to leave. She looked vaguely Latina, possibly some sort of mix of Asian. Except of course that she had no parentage, had been programmed by Hemmingway, just like the house. Her figure seemed impossibly pornographic, long expanses of light brown skin finishing underneath a Victorian-style maid's outfit; the erotic kind, naturally: all frill and lace and barely there at all.

Hemmingway watched her go. "I know you don't approve, Starfire. But she gives me great pleasure."

"I'm sure she does," snorted Selina, whose online handle was Starfire. Best not to use your real name at any point in these sorts of dealings.

"I suppose I walked into that, although that's not what I meant." He paused. "But on the other hand, it's also not untrue." He paused again, chuckled. "I've always found that to be the greatest part of experiencing virtual sensation, don't you think? Living out one's fantasies."

"I find it disgusting, honestly," Selina said.

"You've never indulged?"

"Not once. The web is for business, Hemmingway."

Hemmingway sat back and sighed heavily, sipping from his cup of tea. "Oh, my dear Starfire. You're missing out. If not to please some deep-seated sexual deviancy, then I'm sure you could find other uses for the *simulation* than *business*. Look at me – the only limit to my happiness is the capability of my imagination to conjure new fantasies, and my brain to code them."

"I don't have time for that kind of bullshit, and anyway, I don't know how you can enjoy something that you know is fake," she said, taking another sip of the simulated Earl Grey. "Although I suppose your fake tea is pleasant enough."

"The only way that you can ever *have* time, is if you *make* time. Now, as to how I can enjoy something which, as you've so ineloquently put it, is *fake....* Well, I guess we could have a whole conversation about sensory perception and what makes reality. But I don't suppose you're back so soon looking to discuss the philosophy of the digital?"

She set the tea down. "I'm planning an expedition and in need of personnel for it."

"Oh my, an expedition? Starfire, I would venture to say that the credentials I provided got the job done, then, and you found what you were looking for on that website?"

"Don't get a big head, Hemmingway, but yes. I found something. Not what I was looking for, but something."

"Very good," Hemmingway clapped once, face aglow. "I was rooting for you, you know."

"Come on, we both know that once you had my money, I was out of your mind."

Hemmingway looked wounded, but the expression was fleeting. "You'll think what you want, I suppose, regardless of what I have to say on the matter. As for this expedition, shouldn't you be going through some sort of university protocol to put a dig together? I'm not sure what I can help you with, here."

"It's former Greek territory, off the coast of Turkey. I can get labor cheap once we're there, but I'll need muscle."

Hemmingway shuddered and took a sip of his own tea. "Dear me, that's dangerous territory. I know you can handle yourself, but I still hate to think of you getting taken prisoner by some fringe terrorist organization, or imprisoned by remnants of the Greek government and sold into slavery."

Starfire laughed. "Your concern is touching, but that's why I've come to you. Put me in touch with someone who can protect my poor, delicate person. Someone who doesn't mind going out of the country."

"The cost for someone like that," Hemmingway said slowly, "would be considerable."

"As would your finder's fee, no doubt."

He shrugged and nodded at the same time as if to say "yes, of course."

"Well I've been funded, but I'm not loaded. Can you find me someone good, that I can afford?"

"That's a pretty tall order, Starfire. Someone really skilled, with enough training to keep you alive in such a violent part of the world wouldn't normally come cheap. So, someone desperate then. Someone skilled and desperate." Hemmingway paused and took another sip of his tea. "People like that don't just stroll in off the street Starfire, but for you I'll see who I can drum up."

SELINA

Selina stepped out of the rain and into the coffee shop, water soaking her pants down to her legs and her shoes down to her toes. It sloughed off of her and onto the floor. When she stepped fully through the door, an alarm rang and the security guard moved forward. He towered over her in his alloyed body armor, an expensive and wicked looking gauss submachine gun in his hands. He had not pointed it at her yet. Over the whole suit of armor had been draped the green and white apron characteristic of this particular coffee chain, an article of clothing shared by the baristas behind the counter as well.

"Please place your firearm in the bin to your left," he instructed her in bored monotone. She placed Maurice's old handgun in and it slid shut; the conveyor buzzed once, and a fresh bin slid forward for the next armed patron. She eyed the rack of gun bins. Most of these were empty – it tended to be corporate cube workers that frequented such places, and these were seldom armed because they seldom left the areas of the city protected by guards with alloyed armor and expensive weapons. But there was a gun in the bin beside hers, an old-looking revolver, triple the size of her stun gun. If a gun could be a dinosaur, that thing fulfilled all of the primary characteristics of dinosaurs: Age, size, and clumsiness. Probably belonged to her guy. Hemmingway had said the man would be relatively cheap, after all.

Selina hoped he'd be worth what she did have to pay him. She hoped he was reliable, and wouldn't start any kind of fights or try to pull anything with her. Not that she was particularly worried, what with her stun gun still nestled safely in its holster beneath her jacket. Such a weapon was designed to fool the rudimentary equipment installed in a place like this, and it reassured her that she could handle anything if Hemmingway's guy turned out to be something other than was promised.

She surveyed the rest of the space. A few green-clad baristas. A number of suit-and-tied men and sharply dressed women in pantsuits clustered around small round tables, sipping from recycled paper cups.

Sharp white walls loaded with images of folksy villagers growing coffee beans in far off countries set off the green-tiled floor. Each tile sported the coffee shop logo. Behind the counter, the baristas seemed largely inactive. They took orders from the short line of patrons – humans taking orders verbally had come back into vogue recently – and then pressed buttons on the monstrous contraption behind the counter. It chugged and churned for a brief moment, venting steam and hissing, before spitting out a recycled paper cup full of something hot.

One thing was clearly out of place in this space. Or rather, one person. In the far corner of the room, up against the wall, no drink in hand and fiddling around on an old-model PCom that didn't appear to even have 3-D rendering, sat a middle-aged man. He wore a faded black tie and a threadbare button-down shirt. On the chair behind him an old, past-century beige trench coat that had certainly seen better days. A black hat, wide-brimmed, rested soggily on the head above his weathered face. He seemed long and thin, but sinewy too. Strong enough, she supposed. This was obviously Hemmingway's guy.

A little old for her taste, but if that was his hand cannon in the bin, and he could handle himself in a fight, that would be good enough.

They made eye contact, but then the guy looked away. Probably recognizing her as out of place like him, but unsure if she was the contact. She decided to let him stew a bit. Went to the counter and ordered a couple of beverages. Paid way too much – more per cup than the price per dose of your starter street drugs – and then collected them from another barista whose job, apparently, was simply to remove the cups from the belt and place them in the hands of the customer.

She took them over to the corner of the room and sat beside the man.

"*You're* Starfire?" he said, groaning and leaning back in his chair. "You gotta be kidding me."

"Not a great way to start out a job interview," she replied, setting both cups down on the table between them.

"Job interview? Please. If you had the money to hire some real muscle you'd be conducting job interviews among qualified candidates instead of talking to the likes of me," he said, too loudly.

She looked around, noticing a number of sidelong glances. She felt her face flushing, this stranger treating her like a kid when it was her with the power here, not him, all these corporate drones eavesdropping, this the most exciting thing to happen to them outside a Real-D experience in years.

"But you're talking to me," the man continued, leaning forward again. "Which means you're as desperate as I am." He took a sip from his coffee. "Good stuff. Can't have a smoke in this god-forsaken town, it's too wet to get anything to light, but this is a good substitute."

She slapped the table, hard. "Quiet down," she hissed. "You're making a scene."

He raised his hands, placating.

"And I'm the one with the money here, which means this *is* a job interview. There's plenty of desperate men in the city, but not plenty of women paying you to leave it. So you can sit back and shut up, or you can get up and walk the hell out of here."

He did sit back, and he kept his mouth shut.

"Better." She paused. "Tell me your name," she said.

"Gash."

"Gash? That's not a real name."

He laughed, coarse as the ancient pavement on the downtown sidewalks where Selina had been raised. "Unlike 'Starfire,' right?"

"Fair point. My real name is Selina. Yours?"

"Nagash," he said through clenched teeth. "Never mind all the questions you have about my parents, and what they were smoking. I go by Gash."

"Gash it is," Selina said, sipping from her own cup. Hot chocolate, sweet and rich with the flavor of real cocoa.

"Let's talk business, Selina," Gash said.

Later, their cups empty, their agreements made, and the conversation expired for the moment, they sat in silence and watched the buzzing dance of normal life going on around them. Selina had quickly realized that this dance was foreign to both of them. The man had been a private investigator in Seattle, a metro full of corporate security agencies and investigation teams. A private investigator, much like Gash himself, seemed a thing of the past, and he had the demeanor of one permanently out of place. There was little need for this service in Jacksonville, certainly. Here, if someone had wronged you, you found out yourself and sought street justice at the tip of a blade or the barrel of a gun. Unless of course you were a part of a corporation, and then naturally that security network would seek out and arrest the offending parties, seize their assets or force them into indenturement. Or have them killed.

As if on cue, the door opened and the alarm buzzed again. A thin olive-skinned man with black hair and a black tactical jacket walked through. The green-aproned, armored security guard approached the new arrival, and made his usual demand. Instead, the black-clad operative held out a PCom, projecting in holograph what was clearly a corporate warrant. It looked from where Selina was sitting to be a WalCo warrant, and below it very clearly could be seen Gash's weatherworn face.

He had mentioned there was a corporate warrant out on him and that he'd just dealt with an assassin recently. But he had not specified WalCo, and the fact that another had arrived so soon after the first concerned her greatly.

It didn't matter, she decided quickly. She'd chosen to employ this man, Gash, and she needed him as much as he needed her. He'd already risen to his feet, but she could tell from his stance that he was unarmed, hadn't kept anything hidden when he came through the security door. He had presumably chosen this place because it was public and well-guarded. But had not considered that a corporate warrant would be all a corporate operative needed to carry out a contract on what would otherwise be protected property. And now that he'd been disarmed, he was exposed.

"Nagash Jensen," the man said, his voice high-pitched and yet full of gravitas. "You are found guilty of treasonous crimes inflicted against the free market and against WalCo, and sentenced to die."

He drew a large pistol, almost the size of the armored guard's SMG, and pointed it at Gash. The thing, she could tell from the massive battery pack and the soft hum as it powered into ready mode, was a laser gun. Destructive and ostentatious, such a weapon was not used primarily to kill. Though it did kill quite efficiently, it was employed mostly by people looking to make a statement. Evidently WalCo was looking to make a statement. Selina had not asked her former P.I. what he did to draw a corporate warrant, but she resolved to do just that when this was over.

Before the assassin could fire, Selina found her feet and, stun gun in hand, she fired twice. Both shots found their mark, and two micro-darts pulsed in the WalCo contractor's chest. He looked down, waited for them to stop, and then pulled them out. They clattered to the floor, spent, and the assassin grinned. Clearly augmented. Great.

She barely had time to dive away from the laser pistol's first blast. She heard a whining sound like something out of an old video game, and her chair exploded into splinters. She found her feet again and looked to her attacker, just as Gash charged him head-on.

"Come on, asshole," he roared. But there was simply no way he'd get there in time. The contractor was about to bring that weapon back around and blow Selina's new hire's heart out of his chest. This wouldn't do. She flipped the dial to lethal. Before the voice could finish warning her, Selina laid her finger heavy on the trigger, squeezing over and over again, emptying the clip. Seven micro-darts dumped amperage into the augmented assassin, and not even his dampeners or his stun-resistant neurons or whatever he had could hold back the tide of electricity that coursed through his body. He fell back to the floor, spasming violently. The harsh tang of charred flesh over-rode the carefully crafted coffee aroma, and someone screamed. The patrons had all been distilled by the brief violence into the corners of the room, afraid to try to escape, afraid to stay in their seats. They clung to the walls as though this somehow made them safer.

The armed guard now had his SMG leveled at Selina, and she returned the favor with her stun gun. The logo on his apron seemed ridiculous in context of the standoff, and she laughed. Why hold it in, she thought. The crazier he thought she was, the more likely he'd let them walk out.

"You did your part," Selina said. "You allowed this man into your establishment to fulfill his warrant. Past that, your company has no part in this. Do you really want a bloodbath in your store? How will corporate view such a thing? The patrons here have been subjected to enough disruption already, wouldn't you agree?"

The guard said nothing, but did seem to be wavering. "Besides," Gash chimed in from just to Selina's right. "How well insulated is your alloy armor? It's great for stopping conventional and heat-based small-arms fire, but what kind of voltage can it stand up to? You saw what the young lady's micro-darts can do, do you really think your armor will disperse enough to keep you alive?"

"Fine," the guard said. "Collect your weapons and leave. But if you so much as think of pointing those weapons at me or anyone else in here, I'll turn you both into hamburger meat."

Selina and Gash circled the guard, and at the door collected their respective weapons. Gash shrugged into his trench coat, eying the slain assassin's gear. *Don't do it.* He didn't, fortunately, and Selina slid Mauricio's weapon and her own stun gun slowly into her pocket. As they were turning towards the door, the guard spoke once more. "Oh yeah, and ma'am, you're officially banned for life for violation of store firearm policy regarding hidden weapons."

She gave him an exaggerated thumbs up, the adrenaline still coursing through her as she stepped out into the downpour once again.

SAGE

The Paris Metro car jostled Sage into Hiroyuki, and then back into the young woman standing on their other side. Black stone walls rushed by on the other side of the glass window. Sage produced their PCom and tapped a few keys.

"I have a surveillance unit attached across the street from the safehouse, let's have a look and see if Gerard's made it there yet, shall we?"

"Fortuitous," Hiroyuki said. "But why didn't you bug the safehouse itself?"

"Because these people are paranoid. I'm sure someone sweeps it regularly, and if they found my bugs, my only lead would be so much smoke and dust."

They tapped in the passcode; their PCom found the frequency for the surveillance unit and connected to it. It powered up. The unit was still in working order. Six months since Sage had placed it, and the unit had been soaking up solar rays with its micro-panel, preparing to be re-activated. The image resolved in a matter of seconds; a closed window in the third story, set into the coarse grey concrete of a cheap apartment complex, the blinds drawn shut.

Sage tapped a few more buttons, and then they was viewing thermal imaging of the same unit. Above and below, plenty of heat signatures indicated that this building bustled with life. Expected in a city as over-crowded as Paris, of course. These signatures didn't matter, though. What mattered, and Sage gestured to the screen so that Hiroyuki could see what they saw, were the two thermal images in the safehouse. Gerard had found his way home, as Sage had predicted, and had enlisted help. A second Hospitaller, a new figure.

"Gerard has help," Hiroyuki said.

"We have a second lead," Sage responded.

"Lead to what? What organization is Gerard a part of? I think it's time you filled me in," Hiroyuki said.

"No time." Sage shook their head. "We're only a few minutes away, we need a plan. We have to take them alive, figure out who the hell that is with Gerard."

"I thought we might go in the front door and arrest them both," Hiroyuki said. "Does it need to be any more complex than that?"

Sage extracted a two-foot long metal tube from their gear bag, handed it to Hiroyuki. "A micro-launcher, ever used one before?"

He nodded.

"Good. This one's preloaded with a nerve gas that should paralyze anyone who breathes it in for up to an hour. The safehouse has only one entrance and exit, but these men are heavily armed and highly trained and I don't want to take any chances. You fire this into the unit from the street, and I'll breach and clean up."

"You want me on the street? It feels a bit like you're trying to ditch me again."

Sage shook their head. "Not at all. I don't want them going out the window when we come in the door. You'll be out there to take them down if they jump. It's only three stories, after all, and they're probably auged."

The metro car came to a stop. Smooth voices announced the terminal in French first, then English, followed by several others languages. Sage and Hiroyuki stepped out and joined the throng headed for the surface. Neon images projected from the concrete ceiling danced and spiraled above the Metro riders, advertising anything from cigarettes to Real-D porn experiences to antiques. The promise of commerce, animated and bright. Not the Paris Sage had known briefly as a child.

They emerged into the day, the bright sun once again a razor cutting through Sage's eyes. They wondered if they had a concussion from being struck on the head earlier, but set aside the thought. No time for dizziness. No time for weakness. The iron had not been this hot since Sage had begun pursuing Gerard four years ago, and they intended to strike.

Outside the building, Sage dropped their gear bag to the sidewalk. From within, they withdrew two large gauss pistols, already fully loaded.

Hiroyuki eyed these. "What happened to taking them alive?"

"I hate stun guns," Sage almost apologetically. "Anyway, I know how to aim for the knees if I need to. It shouldn't matter, that gas will paralyze them within seconds."

And then, because they had reminded themself, Sage drew a small breather out of the gear bag. It clamped directly to their face, the adhesive forming a seal with their skin that could be released at the press of a button.

Next from the gear bag, Sage produced a small case. Within, two earbuds, one for both of them. Each placed the bud in the left ear. Sage silently mouthed the words "testing one two." The earbud picked up the vibrational patterns of the sub-vocalized words, transporting them into Hiroyuki's ear. He gave the thumbs up, they were live. People were giving the agents a wide berth now, steering clear of whatever was about to go down.

One last quick look at their PCom to confirm that the two signatures were still both present, and then Sage was on their way towards the door. A firm polycarbonate *click* signified that Hiroyuki had deployed the stock and trigger for the micro-launcher, readying it to be fired.

"On my signal," Sage mouthed, before slipping into the lobby of the apartment building, guns in hand.

Inside, the front desk agent slouched way back in his chair, lost in a stupor. Tripping on something. One of the new hallucinogenic eyedrops, most likely. Not the sort of apartment building with top notch concierge service, but then, cheap was all most folks could afford.

Sage took the stairs two at a time, and eased through the door into the third floor hallway. They had been here before, and remembered it all clearly. The moldy pink carpet, the horrendous green wallpapering, peeled off in more places than not. The stink of wetness, of rot, of time gone by. The safehouse, number 303, third door on the right. A door like any other. The culmination of four years hard investigation, of partners lost and public disgrace in the Lyons office, of near-misses and dead bodies, of sleepless nights and long hard days.

Sage stood beside it. Mouthed one short word. "Now."

And then a faint tinkle through the insulated door – the grenade crashing through the window. Before the men inside would have a chance to react to this breach, Sage put a gun to the door's lock and fired. The magnetic projectile launched at extreme velocity, instantly contacting the door lock. It blasted through the hard steel in a shower of sparks, and the door swung open, Sage stepping smoothly through, taking stock in a blink.

Gerard was rising from the stained blue sofa already. His red overcoat flapped in the gas rising from the canister at his feet. In the chair across from him, another man, much larger, had not begun to move yet. Slower reflexes, it seemed, but he was a behemoth. Obviously augmented; crude, but probably highly effective. His arms and legs appeared to be metal, artificial steel-alloy muscles bunched and ready for action. A camo jacket and shorts covered the rest of him, and an assault rifle rested on his lap.

Sage had a gun pointed at both men by the time they'd found

their feet. Gerard breathed easily in the gas, and the other man calmly held his own breath while producing a breather much like Sage's from a bag at his side.

Shit. First of all, Sage had not stumbled onto a second lead. Gerard had evidently hired a merc; the camo and chrome augs weren't really the Hospitaller's style. But the man looked brutal, clearly a trained killer. Gerard was auged too, if he was breathing the nerve gas without turning blue and passing out. Sage already knew this – the Knights liked to enhance themselves – but they had underestimated the scope. Probably a number of subtle improvements lived beneath Gerard's skin, genetic enhancements and sub-dermal implants.

Gerard looked to his hired muscle. "Outside, this one clearly has a partner or some kind of backup. Get out there and clear us a path. I'll deal with this agent: She's been a thorn in my side for far too long, and it's going to end now."

"I'm not a she," Sage growled. "And if either of you pricks move –" Before they could finish the thought, though, the merc was two steps towards the window. Much faster than anticipated. Sage fired, the handguns kicking and the blue streaks of magnetically propelled flechettes passing through air formerly occupied by camo-bound metal muscles. He was too god-damn fast. He crashed through the window, broken glass erupting outwards like tearing paper, the shards flashing with a few of the sun's errant rays, and he was going to rip Hiroyuki apart; Sage hadn't prepared him for a fight like this. Hadn't expected it.

Before Sage could re-align their weapons towards Gerard, he was moving. He produced a pistol of his own, an older gunpowder weapon, and dove for cover behind the sofa. Sage hesitated. The gauss weapons would penetrate the sofa as though it was a holographic projection, they could easily take out the Knight from here. But they wanted to take Gerard alive. There was so much he could tell them about the Hospitallers, about the war with the White Lotus, about all the lives he'd taken so far.

More than that, taking Gerard alive wasn't just about intel. It was about redemption. Would he have anything on him that would validate their story? Unlikely. Sage needed the man alive, or they would never be anything more at Interpol than a second tier agent with great skills who wouldn't stop chasing a mad conspiracy theory.

In a mere second of hesitation, Sage had opened themself up to attack. Gerard popped out from behind the sofa and fired off three shots. These struck home, throwing Sage backwards onto the floor, the impact jarring their teeth and bringing back the haze of cotton clouds around their brain.

Fortunately, they'd all hit Sage's chest, impacting the nano-weave vest they wore beneath their shirt. Bulletproof. But Gerard didn't know that. That bought Sage half a second of time, Gerard turning and casually preparing to follow his merc out the window.

They sat up quickly, taking careful aim for Gerard's right knee. Cripple him, but leave him alive. That was Sage's best bet at this point. They squeezed the trigger, and in that moment a wave of nausea and dizziness flooded their brain, and Sage's world was spinning, and the gun kicked in their hand and the streak of blue lanced Gerard not through his knee but through his back, a fountain of blood erupting through the window as Gerard slumped to the floor of the safehouse and did not move.

Sage struggled to rise, stumbled over to Gerard. Checked his pulse – nothing – and then stepped over his body to the window. The merc would have made short work of Hiroyuki, but would the beast of a man be coming back up for Gerard, or making a break for it?

Sage leaned out to look, and saw Hiroyuki sitting, cross-legged and unperturbed, beside the body of the monstrous mercenary. The head rested at an unnatural angle, and mechanical fingers twitched in the absence of controlling signals from the connected brain.

Hiroyuki had won, had come away unscathed and snapped the big man's neck like a pencil. Sage had definitely under-estimated their new partner. He waved up. "Did you get him alive?"

Sage shook their head. They was glad they'd both survived, and unconcerned that the merc was dead – he wouldn't have had a thing to shed on the case – but crestfallen that they'd missed their shot on Gerard's knee. Sage definitely had a concussion, but that didn't matter. The only chance Sage had of connecting the murders to the Knights of Malta, and a stupid concussion had taken it away. Marksmanship was one of Sage's strengths, so the failure stung deeply.

Didn't matter. Sage always strove not to live in what could have been, but what was. And what was in this moment consisted of a dead Knight that they had been pursuing around the Mediterranean for four years. A killer wanted for seven different murders. Sage had won. Perhaps they would get lucky. Perhaps Gerard had something interesting on his person.

Sage rifled through the dead man's pockets. The first thing they found were shuttle tickets for a flight to Rhodes in two days. Promising. The Knights of Malta had been headquartered on Rhodes once, many centuries ago. There must be something to this. Sage kept looking. Not much else on Gerard's person aside from a fake identity and a credit chip, loaded up with credits. This Sage pocketed, already thinking ahead to their next move, a move that might take them off the Interpol payroll altogether. This case would officially be over, after four years. Sage wouldn't have an excuse to continue investigating the Knights. Their supervising officer wouldn't consider any talk of shadow wars or secret organizations within the respectable Sovereign Military Order of Malta. There would be a new case and that would be it.

Sage couldn't handle this. There were dark forces at work, and people would keep dying. Perhaps innocent people, collateral damage in a war that the rest of the world seemed oblivious to. They would have to tell Hiroyuki: He'd earned himself the right to know what his new partner's plans were, at least in the abstract.

From there, Sage had two days. Two days to prepare for a flight to Rhodes, to a lawless part of the world where they would have to keep their wits about them at all times. Where they would be chasing a dangerous organization down unknown paths, and without backup for the first time. Two days to hit up contacts one last time, to shake down the streets and run the shadow networks and learn what the word was on the little island of Rhodes.

SELINA

One down, one to go. Selina had her muscle, now she just needed an assistant. This part might be harder. She needed someone savvy enough in the archaeological world to help her with the academic side of things, but not savvy enough to spot her fake credentials or see through them to realize that she'd never received a real education. Preferably someone familiar with the Greek culture, familiar with the eastern Mediterranean Sea. Someone who could handle themselves in a scrape, because even with Gash, Selina knew, this would be a rough place to work.

And most importantly, someone willing to work for free. That would be the rub. Her budget was tapped out. After hiring Gash, and factoring in the cost to rent the equipment and hire the labor in Rhodes, she couldn't afford to hire anyone else. Not that this would be viewed as unusual. For a position like this, it would be common to draw no salary, to be paid in room and board and experience. One of the many reasons Selina had been denied access to the real academic world of archaeology; with the death of her parents, she could never afford to work for free.

Hemmingway wouldn't be of help here. This wouldn't be his area of expertise. But Selina had put out some calls for applications on the day she got approved for funding, and a number of would-be hopefuls had responded.

Gash had been understandably eager to leave the city, but she needed another day or two to interview assistants, and so he'd gone back to his seedy hotel to await Selina's call.

Setting up her meet with Gash in the coffee shop had been a prank on Hemmingway's part, she knew that now. But nonetheless, she was grateful now, sitting in a different brand of coffee shop. Coffee shops were the neutral place of choice for legitimate business, and as far as these assistants were concerned, this was as legit as business came. So this was the logical place to bring her interviewees, one by one, to sort through them. And with just an hour's worth of familiarity, she possessed a bedrock from which to fake it like she interviewed potential assistants here all the time. Like she'd been interviewed here as a potential assistant herself, once upon a time, some few years before. She could not so easily be recognized as out of place among the corporate drones and occasional university student that passed in and out of the establishment.

This particular chain lacked the pedigree and historical name recognition of the one from which she'd been banned for life, but shared the same baristas, security guards, and beverage selection. Where the other guys wore green aprons, these guys wore red aprons. The layout even felt identical, shamelessly stolen no doubt. This place lacked only the emphasis on folksy coffee bean harvesters, the pictures on the wall having been replaced with strangely abstract modern art. The drinks were still served in recycled paper cups, though the fact that they had been recycled had not been highlighted quite as much in the design.

The first of her interviewees each brought a cup of coffee for her to the table and then proceeded to wax on at great length about their academic strengths and their love of ancient history. They bored her, these middle children of middle-class corporate wage-slaves. These were the family rebels, diverging from their comfortable free-market lives to live slightly less comfortable academic lives. They'd be dead weight in Rhodes.

The fourth candidate that took a seat across from her did not come bearing gifts. He looked scrawny, but in his eyes Selina could see something familiar. An edge. The sort of thing brought about not by living, but by surviving. His brown hair had been artfully tousled and he wore the same sorts of clothes as the others, sleek synth-denim pants and button down shirts. His application looked the same, more or less, as the others. According to the paper, his name was Frederick Almond, from Detroit originally. Well, that explained the edge. Detroit was probably more dangerous than Rhodes.

He reached out to shake Selina's hand after he'd seated himself, accidentally knocking her cup over. Fortunately, it was empty.

"Ah, shit," he said, trying to catch it as it fell, but only succeeding in knocking it entirely off the table, and sending it skittering halfway across the red floor of the coffee shop. It came to rest at the feet of a couple of teenage girls wearing McDonald's University polo shirts. They giggled as he bent awkwardly to extract the cup from beneath their table without letting his head get impolitely close to their legs. Then, he resumed his seat, placing the coffee cup firmly back where it had been before.

Selina tried to stifle a laugh.

"That's empty," Frederick said. "You probably didn't need it back."

Selina shook her head, her most important-looking business grimace painted across her face.

He shrugged, his hand halfway outstretched for the cup, presumably to throw it in the recycling bin, but then he thought better of it given the initial success he'd had with reaching across the table. Eventually, he settled in, stopped moving, and for the first time made eye contact with Selina.

"Hi," he said.

"Hello," Selina said, a bit of a grin slipping through her carefully constructed face. "Frederick Almond?"

"That's me," he said, arms crossed with his hands tucked safely away in his armpits.

"Can I call you Fred?"

His face changed for just a second, something firm sweeping quickly across his features and then evaporating before she could really get a feel for it. "No," he said simply.

"Okay," she said, taken aback. To regain her balance, she spent a moment studying his application. "Here's the deal," she said eventually, looking back up. "I've been listening to people drone on about their academic achievements for hours. Let's take a different path here. I'm assuming you're qualified for this kind of work for the time being, and we'll double back and confirm that if needed."

"Fair enough," Frederick said.

"Instead, tell me about your life in Detroit, and why you're a good fit to take a position on a dig in a dangerous part of the world like Rhodes."

"My parents were mid-level executives in the Detroit Renovation project that Ford undertook ten years ago. Simply put, they were killed in gang violence when my brother and I were still teenagers. We were too young for Ford jobs, so they kicked us out of the corporate housing. All we had was each other and the life insurance money, so we got a place in the city and survived. I liked to read history books before bed. I guess it made me feel better to know that the world has always been a violent and shitty place.

"We had enough money to send me to college here in Florida, and we still have enough for a few more years. I'm hoping to teach when I've got enough experience, so that when the money runs out he and I can still live without resorting to a life of crime.

"I'd say I'm a good fit because I survived the streets of Detroit for four years, but I also have a good education and the background to be of help on the dig."

Selina liked him. Frederick seemed to have more going on beneath the surface than he was letting on, but then, anyone that had the edge she needed with the academic background she wanted would be carrying extra baggage.

"You're going to need to prove to me you've got the knowledge for this expedition, I've got a little verbal quiz for you to take."

"No problem," he said.

"Assuming you're going to pass that, I only have one more question for you. Can you be ready to leave tomorrow?"

He blushed and looked away, before looking back at the table in front of him. "Yes," he said.

"Easy there, rosy cheeks," she laughed. "You still have to pass my test first."

SAGE

"I have lived countless lives, Sage. I've been a beggar and I've been a lord. I've been a Chinese sailor and I've been a shepherd in the mountains of Japan. I've fought in wars throughout the centuries. When you've died as much as I have, death holds little mystery, little consequence."

Sage shook their head, grabbing the cold beer and taking a long drink. "I get it. You believe in reincarnation. But none of that helps me understand how you were able to take that mercenary apart so hard."

"I don't just believe in reincarnation. I remember each of my past lives in vivid detail. I've been trained in the ways of martial arts in many of them." He sipped his own beverage, some kind of canned tea-product lettered with Chinese characters that Sage could not read.

The bustle of the Parisian bar formed a sort of cocoon around them. The bar crammed every sort of person imaginable into a small space, most smoking out of retro vaporizers – never mind the enhanced highs and mitigated lows you got from a derm, they were in it for the spectacle of breath, the smoke rising in the bright neon lights flashing from ultramodern vending machines. These sold anything from sexual paraphernalia to books, which were briefly back in vogue. Everything you could want, available for sale on the walls of the bar, except beverages. For beverages you had to go to the bar itself, order from the human bartenders. Tip well. A business model that had not changed in centuries.

"Well, that sounds like bullshit to me. But I can't argue with results, can I?" Sage slammed back the rest of the beer and ordered another with a wave of their hand at the bartender.

"Most people feel the same. I understand."

"Listen, Hiroyuki. We haven't been partners for very long, but I figure after today I trust you, and I owe you the truth."

Hiroyuki nodded, sipping from his can of tea and watching Sage through veiled eyes.

"Four years ago, my first big case, four Chinese nationals were found dead in a Roman motel. Executed. My then partner and I assumed this was a case of two organized criminal organizations running afoul of each other. Each of the victims sported a tattoo somewhere in their person. A white lotus."

Hiroyuki's eyes flashed briefly. "The Order of the White Lotus, the original Chinese secret society. Spiritual predecessor to the Triads. A logical investigative leap."

"Except," Sage continued, "that these four men had no ties to the Triads or any other criminal organization. They had no history, no known associates, nothing we could use."

"Mysterious," Hiroyuki said, setting down his empty can of tea just in time to pick up another as the bartender placed it in front of him. "What other leads did you have?"

"There was a witness. The front desk clerk gave a description to a sketch artist. But we turned up nothing else. The case grew cold. For a year we closed other cases, and that first one continued to haunt me – I hate failure, you see, and had already admitted defeat.

"Until Agent Renoir caught a case in London, a Chinese woman whose brains had been blown out in a dark alley. She had the white lotus tattoo, and CCTV caught a man fleeing the alley. A man in red, whose face matched the sketch from the Roman motel. He passed the case off to us, as it was obviously the same MO as that first case in Rome. We were able to track him using various CCTV feeds. He had killed the woman and gone directly to the British library, of all places. A librarian had helped him find a massive text, a history of the Knights Hospitaller. You know this organization?"

Sage drank deeply from the second beer. They hated telling this story to others, it always came off like a wacky conspiracy theory.

Hiroyuki peered at them. "Yes," he said eventually. "Though I don't know much. A military order like the Knights Templar, right?"

Sage held up a hand, rose to their feet, and stepped a few paces to one of the nearby vending machines. Slotted their credit drive into the machine's interface, tapped a few keys, and slotted the drive out again. The vending machine spit out a pack of nicotine derms, which Sage collected from the opening at the bottom. Unwrapped the tear-away plastic from two, and placed one on each bicep. Rolled the burgundy cotton sleeves of their shirt back down, and returned to the bar stool. Finished the beer and ordered a third. This would be a hard night. But already the nicotine had flooded their system, soothing frayed nerves and bringing on a sensation of restless peace.

"Yes," they said finally to Hiroyuki. "Like the Knights Templar. The Knights Hospitaller were driven out of the holy land in the 13th century. They moved around the Mediterranean, from Cyprus to Rhodes and then eventually to Malta. Present day, they're called the Sovereign Military Order of Malta."

"Ah yes, I am familiar," Hiroyuki said. "What a strange thing to do after committing murder, though, taking a trip to the library. That can't be a coincidence."

"Thank you!" Sage shouted, slapping the bar. A few nearby patrons looked over and stared a moment, before returning to their own conversations, their own business. "Thank you," Sage said again, softer now. "We lost the man – who you can probably guess by now was Gerard – after that, and the case went cold again. But I never let up trying to find a connection between the Hospitallers and the White Lotus. And some months later, in Sicily, a Chinese man with a white lotus tattoo was apprehended. He had killed three people there, using a sword of all things, who turned out to be members of the Sovereign Military Order of Malta."

Hiroyuki's eyes grew wide. "Did you interview this man?"

Sage looked away. "No, the tattoo alone didn't prove to be enough evidence for the bosses to give me access. And at this point I had an unsavory reputation as a conspiracy theorist. But I read transcripts of numerous interviews. He never said a thing. Not one word to this day since he was apprehended."

"That is disappointing, to say the least."

Sage nodded.

"I can guess where this is going," Hiroyuki continued.

"Gerard was my last lead. As far as Interpol will be concerned, we just closed a four-year-old murder case for good. Questions won't be asked as to why he did what he did, or if there's anything else larger going on. But I know there is. I've found links between White Lotus members and Hospitallers in half a dozen case files. The body count is extensive, Hiro."

"What can I do to help?" Hiroyuki asked.

"I found two shuttle tickets to Rhodes on Gerard's body today. The Knights Hospitaller were headquartered there for two centuries, it can't be a coincidence. Here's how you can help."

GASH

The shuttle rocked hard, jarring Gash's bones. White knuckling the arm rests and eyes squeezed shut, he forced breath through thinly curled lips.

Beside him, the musical laugh of Selina Kan. "You're not a flyer, huh?" she asked.

He cracked open one eye to look at her. About half his age, but exceptionally beautiful. Deep olive skin, a thin silver hoop pierced through her lip about forty-five degrees from the center. Rich black hair held into a pony tail. Half his age, he reminded himself. Oh, and also his employer. "Had no problems with it when I was younger," he said. "But with age comes wisdom."

"Sure," her new assistant, Frederick, said from his seat by the window. "The wisdom to be afraid of what is statistically the safest way to travel?"

"You keep those thoughts fresh in your mind when some wacko in Anatolia who doesn't approve of commercial air travel has a long-range AA missile battery pointed at us during our final approach to Rhodes," he retorted. Gash didn't like Frederick. Selina needed help with the archaeology part of the expedition, so it made perfect sense that she would recruit an assistant. There was just something about him. Ultimately, Gash had decided, it was a natural distrust of strangers now that his own personal world had gone to shit. Not the kid's fault. He'd tried to set it aside.

"Oh calm down, Gash," Selina said. "It's an unsafe part of the world, but it's not a perpetual war zone. Besides, we splurged for a Delta AmWay shuttle, and everyone knows that DAW aircraft have the best counter-measures."

Selina had apparently been studying some 3-D geographical imagery, and she returned to this when Gash did not respond.

Gash looked around the shuttle. Unassuming beiges and greys decorated the cabin, along with two more rows of empty seats. A total capacity of nine passengers. The charter craft, designed to take passengers to places not frequented by the larger craft, could not have been cheap. Especially to just take three passengers halfway around the world. A bored flight attendant strapped in at the front of the cabin read something on his PCom in 2-D. Probably a book.

It had proven hard to get the man's attention before, but just then Gash noticed a bright orange button set above him beside the air vents. A stick figure image of a man carrying something that looked like a tray of food. He hit the button, and sure enough, a buzzer sounded, wrenching the now-annoyed flight attendant out of his book. He strode over and looked expectantly at Gash.

Gash wanted to rip the ridiculous maroon vest off the attendant's puffed-up little chest, and choke him with it. His stomach continued to insist on doing somersaults inside of him, and he contemplated the potential satisfaction of at least landing a solid right hook. Selina looked at Gash. He took two deep breaths.

"Something for my stomach," he growled.

Without a word, the attendant disappeared into a small cabin towards the front of the shuttle.

"Excuse me," Frederick said, trying unsuccessfully to slip past Selina and Gash without bumping uncomfortably up against them. He almost fell into Gash's lap. "Sorry," he said.

"This is the third time in like thirty minutes that you've had to use the lavatory," Gash grumbled.

Frederick looked away, red-faced. "Something about the biscuits they served on takeoff," he said.

Selina looked concerned. "I didn't have any issues with them."

"Go on, get out of the way," Gash said, shooing Frederick towards the aft bathroom. The flight attendant had just appeared with a small cup of water and a smaller paper cup that cradled two large white pills. When the man was close, Gash grabbed both cups and chased the one with the other, before returning them to the waiting hands of the attendant.

"Anything else, sir?"

Gash didn't like the way the attendant had emphasized the word "sir," but already the meds were soothing his savage stomach, so he merely waved the man away with a "thank you."

"How much longer?" Gash asked.

Selina laughed again. "Four hours or so. We've only been in the air for about an hour. I told you to bring a book or something."

"And I told you I don't really read," Gash replied. "My PCom is for making phone calls and working cases. That's about it."

Selina retorted with something, the look on her facing telling Gash that it fit firmly in the category "smart ass remark." But a wave of exhaustion hit him just then and the words themselves flew directly over his head.

It had been a hell of a month. On the run from WalCo, flushed out of his home city, now on a shuttle to the ass-end of the world for some kind of *archaeology* project, just to escape imminent death. Of course Gash felt exhaustion in each fiber of his being. How strange it would be if he didn't. Now was the perfect time to sleep. His eyes had already closed themselves, after all, so all that remained was to give in to it, to dream. To rest.

SELINA

When Selina's new bodyguard fell asleep mid-conversation, the hackles rose on the back of her neck. Her danger sense told her something was amiss. She realized that their flight attendant had disappeared from his seat in the front of the cabin and now sat directly behind her.

He whispered when he spoke, the affectation of boredom long gone. "Selina Kan. Know that I could kill you where you sit and be long gone before the shuttle landed. Delta AmWay would investigate and find that your sleeping friend there had done the nefarious deed. But that's not my mission."

"Then what is your mission?" Selina regulated her voice. She would show no fear.

"I'm to deliver to you a message, nothing more. You think you know what you're investigating. You think the path you've chosen leads to a new life. You are –"

"You don't know a thing about my path," Selina interrupted.

A brief pause. Selina started to turn in her seat.

"Best to not," the flight attendant said, the threat clear in his voice.

She didn't. No idea what kind of weapon he might have pointed at her.

"Let me tell you what we know of your path. Orphaned as a teen, you made your own life. Expert hacker. We could bring down corporate warrants for data theft on you from three major corporations, including WalCo, the same one that's after your newly hired bodyguard. Chasing your childhood dream of archaeology, you believe you have stumbled upon a conspiracy regarding the destruction of The Colossus of Rhodes. You believe you will find intact pieces of the wonder, and that this discovery will lend you the credibility to attain a full-time position in academia." He paused and took a deep breath. "We know that the day your father died, with his last breath he beseeched you to uncover the secrets in the little journal he'd given you years before."

At the mention of her father and his little journal, she tensed. Very few people knew about the old book, and she'd always wondered how her blue collar father had stumbled upon such a thing. Selina and Gash had been forced to check all of their weapons at the gate, even though this was a private charter. If she'd had a weapon, she'd have spun around and attacked the flight attendant on the spot. "Skip to the point," she growled through her teeth.

"I believe my words fall on deaf ears, but the message I've been sent with is only this: When you arrive in Rhodes, you will wait two days to avoid arousing suspicion. And then you will return home to Florida, your mission a failure. You'll publish this failure to find anything of interest on the little island. And that will be the last time you think of the Colossus of Rhodes or anything else to do with it."

"I'm sensing an 'or else,' at play here," Selina said.

"Or else you will die, of course."

And with that, the flight attendant rose casually, to walk back to his position at the front of the cabin.

"Who the hell do you work for?" Selina asked.

When he looked back, the bored look had returned to his face.

"Delta AmWay," he said, as though the answer were the most self-evident thing in the world.

Who did he really work for? She watched him take his seat. She watched him for a long time: the resumption of his reading, when he returned wordlessly to refill her water, when he took a call from the pilot on the internal phone system. Why did they want her to stop looking into this? Obviously because there was something to it. The man had seemed to believe his message would fall on deaf ears, and it had. They'd inadvertently proven to her what she had only hoped in her wildest dreams. That there was something wrong with the histories, and that she was hot on the trail of something big.

Where was he from? She studied his face. Generic European white. No distinct features. Was he Greek? Probably not. Part of the Knights Hospitaller, AKA the Knights of Rhodes, AKA the Knights of Malta? Best guess was yes. Rembert had alluded to them many times, though never clearly enough to give Selina a really good idea what their involvement was in a 2300-year-old secret war.

Frederick jostled Gash and accidentally elbowed Selina in the shoulder as he returned to his seat. "Sorry," he said.

She didn't look away from the flight attendant.

"Hey," Frederick said, leaning in towards her. "You okay? You look... uneasy.'"

She considered possibilities. She could let Gash and Frederick know what had happened. The three of them could overpower the man with ease. But to what end? Question him? Use him as a bargaining chip? It seemed unlikely that he would reveal anything useful, or that he had enough value to the Knights to be used as a hostage somehow. And then if she told the other two, would they want to bail on the mission? To turn around and go home? She couldn't risk losing everything she'd been working for her entire life. "Everything's fine," she said, waving him off.

Selina closed her eyes and just listened. Gash breathed heavily in and out, the rhythm of sleep. He would be fine, she knew. Frederick settled back into his seat, returning to the game he'd been playing on his PCom, his breaths shallow. She'd hurt his feelings. There would be time for that later.

Selina pictured the deep cobalt of the night sky above, the endlessly rolling midnight of the nocturnal ocean below, the tiny shuttle sandwiched between, roaring at supersonic speeds through the air at 60,000 feet. Far ahead, a few hours away, the Island of Rhodes waited for them, hot and dry. Deep beneath arid earth and Cyprus trees, a mysterious anomaly waited to be uncovered. What would happen when they arrived and continued to pursue the project? Would she be dragging Gash and Frederick to an early death? Or would they share the wealth of a discovery with the potential to reshape the fabric of history? She did not, could not know.

GASH

Much to Gash's surprise, the shuttle took no missile fire on approach to Rhodes. The pilot brought the shuttle in low, and landed them on a hidden airstrip at the opposite end of the island from the city. Gash didn't get a good view of the island on the way in, but there had been a bright flash and distant boom from the direction of the city.

The airstrip seemed abandoned, but a few locals materialized from a squat white plaster structure by a fence to refuel the shuttle while the three of them disembarked.

"Thank you for flying DeltaAmWay," the flight attendant said, waving from the shuttle's ramp down at them. "We are no longer legally or in any other way liable for your safety. Enjoy your stay."

Selina glowered at the man, but Gash had already moved on. The location was a nightmare. To the west, the beach offered no cover. A craggy coastline dotted with tall grasses and small bushes of some kind. The waves of the Mediterranean lapped at the sand, and it might have been peaceful in another life. To the east, rolling hills speckled with rocky outcroppings and tall cypress trees provided countless locations for ambush. Only the squat structure supplied any kind of cover. Fortunately, a vehicle – an old gas-powered Jeep – had been procured by Selina prior to their arrival, and it sat now just inside the airstrip's fence. If their conspicuous presence had not already drawn the attention of someone who meant them harm, it would not be long before they were en route towards the relative safety of anonymity in the city.

Best to move quickly to the vehicle. Gash shouldered his duffle and started in that direction. He sweat rivers in his long coat. A different kind of heat to the monsoon humidity in Florida, here felt like a desert dropped into the ocean. He could actually hear the waves from the coast, but the Martian air of the place left him desiccated after mere moments, the sweat drying almost immediately, only to be replaced by the next droplets in a never-ending stream. He felt his skin begin to shrivel and crack. It would not be long before they felt the effects of dehydration in a place like this.

"I don't get why we didn't just land in the city," Frederick said, hauling an enormous black suitcase across the concrete towards the Jeep.

Selina looked at Gash. He held his hands up in the air as to say "not me."

"Well, for one thing," Selina started, dragging her own two suitcases in the same direction as the others, "this is where the airstrip is. But it's here by design. The city, like all cities just outside the core Middle East countries, will be full of religious extremists. Islamic fighters battling Orthodox fighters battling Evangelical fighters. The regular denizens of the city go under the radar, as long as they don't get caught in a crossfire or catch a stray bullet. But outsiders draw attention from each group. And we don't want a target painted on our backs. Simple enough?"

Frederick nodded in tune to the long strides he took toward the Jeep. "I guess the only difference is that in Detroit, Ford and some of the other corporations protect the airport. No corporations here, eh?"

"No money here, no corps here," Gash growled. "Let's make it quick, smells like an ambush." For good measure he slid the giant hand cannon out of his bag and loaded it as he walked.

At the Jeep he made to hop into the driver's seat, but Selina grabbed his shoulder. She shook her head at him. "You got it, boss," he said, moving around to the front passenger's seat, he in turn bumping Frederick into the back.

The roads, no longer kept up and many decades from their last paving, did not provide a smooth ride. Gash stifled his nausea to the best of his ability. Had to keep an edge. The road rolled and shuddered them past countless potential ambush sites: places for an extremist of some sort to waylay them, or a gang of down-and-outs living in this lawless region to try and make highwaymen of themselves. But with each passing minute, it became more clear that no ambush awaited them.

Surely in a place such as this, someone kept an eye out for unlikely outsiders? People with money, as it were. He shook his head. Failing to come under attack wasn't something to be sad or concerned about. Quite the opposite.

Gash looked at Selina. Alert but relaxed. A half smile trying but not remaining hidden beneath a scowl on her face. "What's got you feeling so good?" he asked.

The smile blossomed fully on her face, soft and dimpled and perfect. Gash looked away.

"This is my life's dream," Selina said. "I can't tell you how long I've waited to be here, the things I've done to make it happen. It feels good, okay?"

"Just don't let your guard down. It doesn't feel right. This place should be a warzone, and yet the only air traffic in the sky doesn't draw a peep."

"It *is* a warzone," Frederick said. "Didn't you see the explosion when we were landing?"

Selina gestured broadly, pointing back at Frederick with her thumb. "Kid's got a point."

The kid *did* have a point. Maybe his skin-of-the-teeth escape from

WalCo had left him paranoid. A place like this would be a warzone, sure, but that didn't mean bad guys were waiting around every corner to ambush the unwary. Gash took a deep breath, the brush and hills blurring as he allowed his eyes lose focus, his attention turning inwards and his focus coming to rest on a distant point far past the horizon.

He'd only been in Florida for a couple weeks, hardly enough to be truly accustomed to the intense and constant humidity, but already the dryness of Rhodes pulled at his skin. It would be hard to acclimate. Thoughts of Florida brought, unprompted and with all the character of a sucker punch, thoughts of Lulu, her slender frame and hard lips. They'd had a purely business relationship, she'd done him a favor after and helped him escape the country. They'd not shared any particularly intimate moments, and she'd seemed content to wave goodbye at the corner outside Hemmingway's place as they parted ways, but there was something about her. Something in her eyes when they'd been on the cusp of goodbye. Probably nothing, but he felt a little heavier now, thinking of her. He'd escaped the States, put enough distance between himself and WalCo that the cost of killing him would presumably exceed the benefits thereof. But instead of feeling freedom, he now felt as though some invisible weight anchored him to the seat of the Jeep, drawing his gaze through the world and into some faraway plane.

Perhaps it had nothing to do with Lulu and everything to do with his dulled edge. Since WalCo, he'd not been himself. Had only survived the first assassination attempt, it seemed, because of an old manual lock. Had only survived the second because Selina had saved him. The old Gash would never have been caught flat-footed, would never have charged an armed gunman with nothing but a battle cry and bare hands. The Gash that had fought his way out of the WalCo labs, *that* was the warrior Gash. The soldier inside him that always appeared in times of peril. The being of pure instinct that had kept him alive in times of battle and times of danger. Where had that version of himself been?

And was that why he longed, with each passing outcropping, each possible hiding place, for attack? For violent combat? It must be, he decided, that he yearned for a chance to find his lost self, a warrior avatar that cared nothing for lost loves and lost lifestyles, that bathed in the blood of his enemies and felt no sorrow.

What did that say of him, that he would wish danger down on these two young kids out of a selfish need to lose himself? What did that say of him, given that he had promised Serena he would find himself a peaceful life of solitary contentment? Perhaps he could never have such a thing.

The Jeep hit a particularly large pothole with a bang, jostling Gash, bring his nose to within inches of breaking on the glass.

"Maybe you should have let Gash drive," Frederick quipped.

"Shut up, Frederick," Selina said, her lilting laugh filling the small space to the brim, filling it to bursting.

SELINA

After arriving in the city of Rhodes, Selina could feel tension draining from each of them in turn. Gash had been coiled the whole ride across the island, expecting a fight that never came. Selina felt good, but had shared some sense of that danger on the road. It seemed too quiet on the island. Frederick had even shown some signs of nerves, though he never stopped telling bad jokes and trying to lighten the mood.

The city looked much like Selina imagined it would have looked a hundred years ago. White buildings – squat rectangles – dominated the landscape. Old gas vehicles lined the sides of the roads, though most seemed to be in a state of disuse. The streets were filled with bicycles, locals riding with heads down. They cruised slowly through the streets, and nobody looked up, nobody made eye contact. Old, dusty solar panels peppered most of the rooftops, rusting conduit running haphazardly down to the sides of buildings, the only thing breaking the illusion of a century's old island paradise.

The changing climate had dropped Rhodes to the bottom of the ladder when it came to economic viability. Not much could be grown here, and the country lacked exports. These people lived hard lives, so of course they didn't much care whether outsiders cruised the streets or not. Like Florida, the place was *hot*. But unlike her adopted home, the place was practically a desert. Sparse vegetation and stunted cypress trees made up the only real greenery on the island, and here in the city even these were missing. Tumbleweeds bounced down the street, occasionally careening off the Jeep as Selina made for the hotel she'd booked two days prior.

She parked the vehicle on the side of the road, and the trio unpacked their bags. The Jeep locked safely behind her, Selina led the way into the hotel. She'd found the place online, didn't really know what to expect. Not a lot of places catering to out-of-country visitors here. Plenty of islands in the Mediterranean for tourists to visit *without* this kind of close proximity to the Middle East.

Inside turned out to be surprisingly pleasant. Two massive fans circulated the air, and it felt almost fresh inside. Beige carpeting, recently cleaned, and unblemished white plaster walls.

"What, no AC?" Gash growled. He could not see Selina roll her eyes. She hoped the proprietor wouldn't be offended.

The man at the front desk shared Selina's complexion, though he was presumably Greek or Turkish. His smile seemed genuine, and when he spoke, his English was flawless. He pretended not to have not heard Gash – a good choice.

"Welcome, welcome," he said. "You must be Selina Kan and associates."

Selina approached the desk and placed her credit drive gently beside the man's old computer terminal. "That's us," she said.

"How long will you be staying?" he asked.

"Indefinitely," Selina said.

"We're archaeologists," Frederick piped in, giddy as a schoolboy now that things were becoming real. She hadn't given it much consideration before now, but evidently Selina was not the only one fulfilling a lifelong dream – Frederick had likely nursed dreams much like hers after the death of his parents and all through school.

The Greek man tried to suppress a smile, but when he slotted the credit drive and tapped a few keys, he lost that fight. To him, Selina felt sure, the sum on the drive amounted to a fortune. Of course, she still needed to find a construction outfit on this island, and hire them to mount a dig. To stay here for the months required and hire the appropriate personnel would *take* a small fortune.

"Excellent, we will debit the funds from your account each night. Please give twenty-four hours' notice before checking out."

Right, Selina thought, *because demand for rooms is so high.*

"The suite of rooms you reserved can be located on the top floor, up the stairs and just to the right. Please enjoy your stay, my friends." He slid the credit drive back across the counter to Selina, almost bowing as he did.

The stairs, like the lobby, featured crisp and airy colors. Nothing offensive. The rooms were furnished cleanly, with the sort of half-sized tempur-recliners and modern art holo-paintings once popular in American hotels during Selina's childhood. Not bad for a place that in all likelihood saw little-to-no business.

The suite featured four rooms connected by a common area. Selina intended to turn the fourth room into a temporary office.

The trio chose their rooms and unpacked gear. When that was done, Selina found her way to the balcony. Up on the third floor of the building, their room overlooked a steep decline towards the beach. The sand stretched down the coast towards the ruin of an old castle. The Palace of the Grand Masters, a leftover from almost a thousand years earlier, when the Knights Hospitaller had occupied the island and become the Knights of Rhodes.

Her breath caught a little in her chest when she saw the famous castle, the disarray of fallen stones asymmetrically artful, the blocky white buildings that ringed the hill beneath it a stark contrast to the deep gray of the citadel itself. On the beach below, a handful of local residents could be seen laughing and playing in the surf. A dog sprinted after a thrown stick.

A cool morning breeze found her on the balcony, fluttering the loose white pants and shirt that she'd changed into. Life had taken such a turn. Would it continue to do so? In this moment of peace Selina could almost forget that her life had been threatened the night before. Almost. Who could actually forget something like that, even living as she sometimes had? Yet she had brought Gash for protection, and if the creep from the shuttle came after them, Selina felt confident that between Gash and her, they had it covered. She had, after all, already handled a Bermuda gang attack and single-handedly taken out a trained WalCo contractor in the last week alone. She would keep her wits about her, and her team would be fine.

SAGE

A sweltering wave of summer heat descended on Sage like a down comforter when they stepped out of the hotel and into the Parisian streets. Immediately the bi-directional lines of pedestrians swept them into motion towards the shuttleport. They felt strange, wearing civilian clothes. A loose-fitting blue shirt, buttoned across the always-useful nanoweave vest, and casual slacks. Not too different from the usual, but as a state of being it didn't feel right.

Going AWOL on Interpol had not been an easy choice. But when the Commissioner called and left a holomail on Sage's PCom demanding immediate debrief on the death of Gerard and his mercenary sidekick, it had made up Sage's mind. They had watched the commissioner speak, the flecks of spittle cascading angrily from the corners of his mouth, and felt only disgust. None of the pride they had originally felt on joining Interpol. People would continue to die because Interpol couldn't imagine that its least favorite andro agent was right about a shadow war between secret organizations.

But Hiro had believed. With little fuss or discussion, Hiro had nodded and accepted that Sage was correct. Did he know more than he was letting on? Was he just trusting? Did he have intuition that past partners didn't, that had allowed him to understand that Sage was correct? It would be impossible to say. When Sage had asked him to stay behind and cover for them, Hiro had only smiled and refused. "You have two tickets, yes?" he'd said, and that was it.

Sage stepped up and into the Paris light rail car that would take them to the shuttleport. They would be meeting Hiro there, and Sage would have backup on their mad quest. The two had considered discarding Gerard's tickets and buying two fresh tickets for themselves, but the tickets were through a private subsidiary of a major American corporation, not known for political machinations or caring too much where money came from. It would be cheaper to bribe the pilot to take them, though clearly neither Sage nor Hiro would be able to pass as Gerard. Perhaps more important than cost, chartering a shuttle to Rhodes would take time. Few corporations would risk an asset with the value of a shuttle in a region known for heavy partisan warfare and random acts of violence without careful planning and consideration. Sage did not care to wait.

As the light rail car lurched forward, the lights dimmed, and holo-ads sprang to life. Directly above Sage's head, a pair of glistening lips, a sultry French voice describing in great and intimate detail the things she wanted to do to whatever listener would come down to Francois' Real-D Parlour, only three blocks from the Eiffel tower. A little further down, a projection of a smiling robot spun a pizza up and down into the air.

Though standing in a crowded train car and bombarded by stimuli, Sage could feel sleep making an attempt on their consciousness. Preparing for this journey had made for a stressful couple of days. Interpol had begun to search for its errant agents; Sage received calls from two old partners, obviously forced by the commissioner, and Agent Renoir, one of few people at Interpol who'd treated Sage with respect. Renoir's call had not come from the home office, and had not shared the scripted feel of their two old partners. He seemed genuinely concerned. Sage simply didn't have time for any of it. The lead was getting cold. They and Hiro had been in separate hotel rooms in distinct parts of the city, an attempt to foil hotline requests for tips regarding an andro and a Japanese man working together. But they had met both days in the library, Sage taking crash courses in Rhodian history while also funneling Hiro required reading on the Knights of Malta.

Now, geared up and educated as well as could be expected in such a short time, Sage and Hiro would meet at the shuttle and fly to Rhodes to see what they could uncover. The light rail pulled to a stop outside the private shuttle terminal out of which the two former Interpol agents would be flying. Hiro waved from the shade beneath a sharp overhang beside the door to the terminal. His eyes smiled as they always did, and his conservative apparel/Buddha tie combination had gone unaltered. This tie featured a purple background and a giant likeness of the Buddha flashing a peace sign. A small rolling suitcase rested at his feet.

"Hiro," Sage said, stepping to the sidewalk, their huge duffle bag slung across their back. "You sure you want to do this? It's not too late for you to go back."

Hiro sighed. "I've told you I plan to help. Let's not talk about going back, but about going forward." He reached for the rolling bag, and the motion sensor picked up the motion, extending with a soft click. They entered the terminal.

The private shuttleport terminal boasted a very different experience than standard air travel. Each of the big airline corps employed dozens of heavily armed guards, and at least two very thorough security checkpoints for air travelers to pass through. Here, Sage and Hiro marched down a long hallway lined with chairs, but with no security checkpoints at all. Some kiosks featured single pilots selling travel as a food vendor might sell synth-beef patties to hungry passersby. Other kiosks clearly belonged to mercenary outfits. Armed men milled about in these areas, outsiders not welcome at all.

Hiro and Sage passed by a number of kiosks before finding themselves standing before a small woman wearing a rather revealing

Hawaiian shirt. Behind her were three separate kiosks, each matched to a corresponding door. A heavily armed and armored guard stood beside each. The sign above the small woman read "Freedom Air: Don't Let Circumstances Tell You Where to Travel."

The woman's smile remained locked on her face from the moment Sage set eyes on her. She turned it on them and Hiro as it became clear to her that they were bound for Freedom Air.

"What can I do for you?" the woman asked from behind her teeth.

Sage handed her the two tickets.

She quickly analyzed them, and looked up at Sage and Hiro, smile faltering. "Which one of you is Gerard deMontaigne?"

Sage leaned in, conspiratorially. "Neither of us. But he wanted us to go in his place."

Hiro nodded amiably.

The woman in the Hawaiian shirt tried to hand the tickets back to Sage, but they refused to take them. "If Gerard wanted someone else to travel in his place, he should have called that into the home office and let us know. We would gladly have changed the names accordingly."

Sage pushed the hand holding the tickets gently back towards the body it was attached to. "Gerard didn't have time for that, I'm afraid. But we understand if there's a last minute fee associated with doing something like that on that same day." They produced the credit chip they'd taken from Gerard's dead body, and held it out to the woman.

A deep silence descended for what seemed like many moments. Sage wondered if this was going to work. And then, the wondering gave way to relief. The Freedom Air agent stepped up to one of the kiosks and typed rapidly for a moment. Then she stepped back, looked back and forth in the terminal as though expecting one of her bosses to materialize out of nowhere, and slotted the credit chip in her own personal PCom.

When Sage received the chip back, they slotted it into their own

PCom, and it asked for authorization to approve the transfer of 200 credits. Expensive, but then, it wasn't their money. The green APPROVE button blinked once and went away once pressed.

The woman ushered the two into one of the doorways. A long walk down a hot tunnel led them out onto the tarmac. "Wait here," the woman said, and stepped out towards the shuttle waiting for them. The pilot, a gruff-looking man in a black jumpsuit, inclined his head towards the woman as she approached. They spoke in hushed tones for a moment, and then the pilot waved Hiro and Sage in.

They stepped up the shuttle ramp, and took two seats. Shortly thereafter, the pilot took a seat across the aisle from Sage, eyes straight ahead, and said nothing for a moment.

The silence grew uncomfortable. Sage was preparing to ask if they were waiting for other passengers – of course they weren't, who would want to travel that close to the Middle East? – when the pilot finally spoke.

"Marie didn't know who Gerard was, the people he worked for. I do. I don't know who you are or what happened with Gerard, but I can tell you're not his people. If you want me to take you, I'm going to need a lot more than you gave Marie."

Sage looked at the man. After years in Interpol, Sage had developed a keen sort of emotional sense. The pilot's emotional state could only be characterized as nervous. Wet-your-pants nervous. Terrified. But of course, not frightened enough to overshadow his greed.

"How much?"

"A thousand," he said. Sage had that and plenty more on Gerard's credit chip. But for that plus the 200 they'd given Marie, they could've just chartered their own shuttle.

"If I give you a thousand," Sage said, "for something I already bought and paid for, I'm going to need information too. Everything you know about Gerard and his people."

The pilot looked away, out the window, for a long time. Then, eventually, he looked back at Sage. The fear practically overflowed.

"Six hundred," he said. "And I don't come out of the cockpit once, we don't share words at all from here to Rhodes."

Sage handed him the credit chip. There wasn't anything this pilot knew about Gerard and the Knights that they hadn't already figured out. Only kind of person Sage needed to pump for info would be a local on the island. But the pilot didn't know that, and his fear had been worth 400 credits to Sage and their cause.

When the pilot returned the chip to Sage, he rose and entered the cockpit. There would be no flight attendant, not on a trip like this. Sage and Hiro would be alone for the brief flight to Rhodes. Enough time for a nap, perhaps. Sage leaned into the forming foam of the synth-leather chair and took a deep, long breath.

GASH

It had not taken long for restlessness to set in. Gash had spent an hour scouring the grounds of the hotel, and discovered nothing amiss. The place seemed legit. Not a lot of other patrons, just a young couple sitting on the balcony of their own room, and an older man napping in a reclining chair in a room just to the side of the balcony.

After, he'd needed to get out. He told Selina he wanted to get a feel for the city, maybe find them some food. Both of those statements were true, in that neither of them were false. But something raged inside of him. He couldn't figure out what or why, and so he walked the streets of Rhodes, agitated. Searching for a danger he sensed somewhere beneath the placid veneer of a city forgotten by time.

The streets and the buildings in them had been left behind in a previous century. Motor scooters running on gasoline whirred past. White plaster buildings lined both sides, well-kept but long outdated. Bored-looking pedestrians strode along at a leisurely pace. Gash saw not one weapon, not one armed guard. Where were the extremists? Where were the bombed out buildings, the tense looks in the eyes of locals that had been conditioned to accept violence as a frightening but everyday aspect of life? This close to Turkey and the country formerly known as Iraq, with a Greek and Christian cultural history as well, it should have been ground zero. Constant warfare.

Gash's pace had slowed; he strolled, as in a dream, into a little outdoor market. Most of the locals looked past him, as though he were a man made of glass. But one vendor, standing behind a stall full of smoked meats, waved him over.

"Good afternoon, sir," he said with a flourish. "You have a look of great hunger about you."

The English, heavily accented but fluent, surprised Gash. In a hotel, sure. But a little market stall in the middle of this bizarre little city? He was tongue-tied.

"We have exceptional lamb skewers. And real chicken! Synth-steak, of course, high-grade product imported from the clinics in Osaka. You are from America, yes?"

Gash managed a nod.

"I bet you have not ever had real lamb before?"

Gash shook his head.

"Then you're in for a treat, my friend!"

When Gash continued not to speak, the man began to look around. Gash felt that something was amiss here. Perhaps not this man, but a feeling had settled into his gut. A feeling he'd learned to trust.

"Sir, perhaps I've mistaken you? Perhaps the hunger is not for food. Perhaps it is... for something else?"

Gash leaned in. "Do I look like a junkie?" he growled.

The man grinned, his teeth almost brown. "Perhaps you do not see yourself this way, but I have known many junkies." His eyes flickered to something just past Gash, and then back to Gash. "And I suspect you are about to receive the thing which you crave. Assuming, of course, that thing is trouble." And with that, the vendor ducked behind his stall. Gash whirled around.

There were two of them, paler white than the locals and blonde-bearded, with red cloaks drawn over bulky frames. One held a shotgun and the other a pistol. They pushed through the crowd which, spotting them, began to disperse quietly.

This was more like it. A crowd conditioned to violence, and doers of violence armed in the street. Not the religious terrorism Gash had expected, but an answer to the question at least. He smiled, wide and toothy. The men slowed, and not just their walk. They'd lost a step, not expecting their quarry to catch on to them nor to seem eager for violence. They hesitated, each motion sluggish. Gash's transformation had begun, the instinctual self superseding the conscious mind.

The men in red moved in slow motion, and Gash had his hand cannon pointed at the first before either of them could bring their own firearms about. The cannon kicked, and a deep red blossom grew out of the pistol-wielder's forehead. He dropped. The shotgun spit in retribution, but too late. Already Gash was running perpendicular to the point of attack. The shot took a chunk of wood out of the stall at waist level, showering the ground with splinters.

He heard nothing. Of course, he heard everything, keenly attuned to the position of the second attacker and the bark of the gun. Beyond that, the patter of footsteps – civilians running away, no danger there – and the sound of a flag whipping in the wind that Gash had not heard before. But nothing registered consciously. He'd been trapped inside his body, his senses co-opted for a greater purpose, watching a slow motion action reel from afar.

He hurdled a patio table outside of what looked to be a local café, shards of glass exploding just behind him as another shot took out the window. Distant screams. Had someone been hit? Tough shit, this was a hard world. If you didn't know to take cover when people started shooting, then you didn't have what it took.

He dove behind a bench. The metal sparked and more wood splinters flew as the shot took a chunk out of it. Gash felt a bit of something wet dripping down his ear. Had a piece of shot ricocheted into his head? Had he just got a splinter of wood in there? No time to check now. A brief lull. The attacker reloading the shotgun, shell by shell. An opening.

Gash popped up, his weapon pointed at the attacker's head. He reconsidered. This was no random act of violence. He'd been singled out for termination by an organization that had the resources to find him, and a desire to kill him. Could this be WalCo, chasing him to the ends of the Earth? It didn't seem likely. That flash of recognition in the meat vendor's eyes spoke of something local, a militia or organization that had put roots down on this tiny island. A reason that the garden variety terrorism had ceased to strike Rhodes as it continued to bring tumult to other cities in the region. Gash could not feel safe, or feel that Selina and Frederick were safe, without knowing who these people were and what they wanted.

He readjusted his aim. The assailant brought back up the shotgun. Gash's hand rocked back with a crack, and an explosion of blood just above the man's right knee saw him crumple to the ground. "Jenga," Gash muttered.

The square was abandoned when Gash took stock. Most of the denizens of the island had cleared out when bullets started flying. This was not the first such firefight they had seen. The meat vendor rose again, smile gone, hands shaking.

Gash looked away from him, towards his prize. Only something wasn't right. A white froth glazed his lips, and he convulsed. Gash didn't even bother to check him out up close. Some kind of suicide pill. Black ops shit, or at least what you'd expect to see in such movies. The scene, grisly enough already, found extra color when the white froth was replaced by gouts of blood, the man coughing violently in his death throes.

"Sir," the meat vendor called, voice shaking. "The Knights would not move against you if they did not know why you were here. And... who you were here with?"

"The Knights? And what makes you think I'm here with anyone?"

"The Knights Hospitaller, the Knights of Rhodes, the Sovereign Military Order of Malta. They've taken up residence in the old castle. They are... at war with another group here on our poor stricken island. As for who you are here with, you cannot be a tourist. We have no tourists here. So you must be here on business. In which case you are either intelligent and did not come alone, or you are a fool who came alone. You do not seem a fool to me."

"Why are knights occupying this island? Why are they attacking me? What the damn hell is going on?" Gash growled, stepping closer to the vendor.

The merchant held his hands up. "Questions to which I am not privy the answers. But I will tell you again, your companions are very likely in trouble. The Knights prefer to divide and conquer."

Gash froze. Selina. His charge. His job, protect the health and well-being of Selina Kan, earn himself peaceful respite in a distant corner of the world. He holstered his weapon and began to run.

"If you survive," the vendor called after him, "come back and try the lamb!"

GASH

The hotel's exterior revealed no signs of a struggle. Nothing amiss whatsoever. But when Gash stepped into the lobby, it became obvious. The man at the register looked up from something behind the desk, looked down, and then did a double take at Gash's face.

"Welcome back," said the receptionist, his greedy smile long gone, replaced by something that flashed briefly behind the mask. He reached for the phone, his words coming too quickly. "Shall I page the ladies and let them know you've returned?"

Gash reached across the counter, white knuckled, gripping the man's collar, pulling him in close. "I can read you like a book, innkeeper. You stink of sweat, and the look of pure frightened shock when you saw me stroll back in couldn't have been any more transparent. You're working with the Knights of what-the-fuck-ever, and you thought I'd be dead by now. Are they up there right now?"

It all came spilling out. Gash had that effect on civilians sometimes. "I'm sorry, they made me. They knew you were coming, and when you came they said you'd either stay for two days or stay indefinitely. And if it was the second one then they'd pay me double whatever you were going to pay to let them know when you split up or were asleep, and give them a copy of the room key." He took a deep breath. "I'm sorry, I'm sorry, but here if you don't work with the Knights, you're against the Knights, and I'm too young to die. Please I'm sorry," he was sobbing now, and Gash let go of his collar. The pathetic wad of him crumpled to the floor and didn't move.

Gash cursed. How long had they been here? Long enough that it would all be long over. He took the stairs two at a time, dreading the scene he would find. Selina and Frederick sprawled out, holes in their heads, unbreathing.

But before he could get his hand around the doorknob, Gash heard a voice. Loud, giving quite a monologue. He listened through the door, which had been left cracked open.

"... again that your bodyguard has already been dispatched. Holding out for his return will earn you nothing but a swift death. If you want to live, you will tell us why you've come to Rhodes, what you've learned, and where you learned it."

The man droned on before Selina or Frederick could answer, but evidently they were alive. The instinctual creature had not yet receded, and now it returned in full force. He peeked through the crack in the doorway. Three more red-cloaked knights stood in a semi-circle around the sofa. Selina and Frederick had not been bound, probably not even searched, given that Gash could not see her stun gun on the floor or in the hands of one of the captors. They were arrogant, these knights. Did not expect much out of an old washed up P.I. and a couple kids. They would learn the hard way, as many others had.

He kicked the door the rest of the way open. It swung inward with a crash paralleled by the deafening crack of the hand cannon in close quarters. The middle knight, in mid-monologue, dropped forward onto his chest from the impact.

The others spun around, a sub-machine gun in each hand, old gunpowder like the first two. Gash ducked back into the hallway just as two streams of bullets chewed through the swinging door and the wall across the hall.

Gash waited a beat, until the firing stopped. He heard a faint voice. "Lethal force mode engaged," it said, and then there were two thumps. The aroma of burnt flesh rode into the hallway on thin tendrils of smoke. He was back through the doorway, and there stood Selina, stun-gun in hand, over all three bodies.

He opened his mouth to speak, but the middle body, the leader, stirred. And Gash saw something, a small cylinder about the size of a hand grenade, in a gloved hand. The knight flipped onto his back and lobbed the thing into the air. It exploded in a flash of radiant light and ear-splitting sonic shock. Gash staggered back into the hallway, and felt himself falling into the wall.

He could not move. The world pulsed white, a piercing ring replacing all normal sound. Gash thrashed around, trying to clear his head enough to move. Impending death loomed. But did not come.

Eventually, Gash's head cleared, and he rose. There were two dead knights in the room, and a broken window. Gash stumbled to the window's edge. Down below, no sign of the leader of the knights.

"Some heavy augs," Gash muttered. "Flashbang dampers, fall impact resistance, enough dermal armor to survive a .44 to the back."

"Gash, Frederick," Selina started, her voice almost sheepish. "I have a confession to make."

She knew, he realized suddenly. She'd known this was coming, or something like. She'd known and done nothing. Perhaps she'd not truly believed. Or perhaps they were on the trail of something huge, something worth the risk.

Anger came, and as quickly slunk away. She'd been trying to get out, too. Out of a shit life she'd been born to or forced into by circumstances. Out of a life on the fringe of a great big machine in which you were either a cog or dregs. Gash had seen it in her eyes the first time, as surely as he'd known it to be in his own. And this was her ticket out. Looking into those big brown eyes now, he knew she thought he would abandon her. A secret this big, he figured, he probably owed it to her. Her secret had almost gotten him killed.

But it hadn't gotten him killed, and he wouldn't abandon her. What wouldn't Gash do to accomplish the same thing, to finally cut the ties on his old life? Finally escape, free and clear, and find that peaceful life Serena had always wanted for him?

He reached out before she could unload all of the words building up in her mouth, grasped her gently by the shoulder. "It's all in your eyes," he said. "It's all okay. Just tell us what we're up against."

SELINA

The proprietor of the hotel cowered in the corner behind the desk when the three of them descended the stairs into the lobby. Selina watched Gash vault the counter and lift the terrified proprietor to his feet.

"We have some questions," Selina said, leaning on the counter. Frederick stood further back, quiet. He'd not had much to say since the attack. Where Gash had forgiven her on the spot for keeping her egregious secret, Frederick had said nothing. But, as the intern, he didn't have much power here. How would he get home without her? She felt bad for him, but dealing with his hurt feelings had to be a back burner issue until they got the whole surviving situation figured out.

"I, I told him," the man said, stuttering, "the Knights forced me. Here, you are with them or you are against them, in which case you are dead."

"So the Knights of Rhodes are in power here?"

"Yes and no," he said, quivering. "Please, I will tell you anything, only call this one off." Gash leaned in close, scowling, his revolver at his side.

Gash looked at Selina. She nodded, and he took one normal-sized step back.

The proprietor smoothed his ruffled clothes, and did what he could to compose himself. Then he looked up at Selina and spoke, the stutter removed – with obvious difficulty – from his voice.

"Thank you. I apologize for my betrayal, and I know I don't rate such courtesy, but thank you nonetheless."

"Talk," Gash growled.

"Yes, of course. You asked if the Knights were in power here, and to an extent they are. They control the city, and hold court in the old fortress. Dozens of them, augmented and armed to the teeth. They are the law in the city, and they keep us safe from terrorists. They do not ask too much, but when they do ask for something, they enforce the request with violence."

"So the Knights *are* in power here," Frederick said, stepping forward.

Selina suppressed a small smile. He was engaging, he was on board. She hadn't lost him either.

"In the *city*, yes. In the countryside is a different story."

"Tell us this story," Selina said softly.

The man gulped. "There is another small army in the countryside. None of us goes out there, because we know they are out there. They are Asian – a Chinese organization, I've heard – and they are seldom seen. When they have been spotted, it's been gunfights and small skirmishes fought against the Knights. The Knights call them the Order of the White Lotus, and offer a generous bounty for us to kill them on sight. Some have left the city to collect this bounty, none have returned. The rumor is they are *digging* out there, though who can say what for?"

"Digging?" Selina asked.

"Like an expedition. A construction company outside the city went out of business many months ago when all of their heavy equipment was stolen, and rumor is that the White Lotus did this."

"What are they digging for?" Selina asked, her heart sinking. No way this was a coincidence. Some other secret organization had come here for the same thing she had, and they did not sound friendly.

The Greek man shrugged. "Nobody knows."

Selina stared at the counter, brain afire. What would a Chinese secret society care about the Colossus? What could they be digging for? She needed time to process this, to consult Rembert's journal. There had not been any mention of a White Lotus organization, but that had been long ago.

"We only have one more question for now," Gash said. "Where can we go where the Knights will not follow?"

"There are many old monasteries, abandoned for centuries but still standing," the Greek man said. "I will show you on a map where there is one on the outskirts of the city. Tourists used to visit it, but nobody goes there now. It should be safe."

A flash of memory struck Selina. Rembert had mentioned a monastery on the outskirts of the city of Rhodes, a hidden room in the basement with clues carved into the wall by a blade. It was this room that had led Rembert to the Colossus' foot. Could this be the same monastery?

"Show us," Selina said.

"And tell us," Gash said, "when the Knights come to retrieve their dead, what will you say of us?"

The proprietor paled. Perhaps he had not thought through the situation properly.

"I'll tell you," Selina said. "You will say that we walked out without a word, that you have no idea where we went." She paused, watched the color drain fully from his face. "You will do this because if we have to kill more Knights because of you, we will return here. And I'll let *him* have his way with you." Gash didn't move, but the proprietor cringed nonetheless.

"Yes, of course," he said.

He showed them the location of the monastery. The one, Selina hoped with sudden passion, that Rembert had been in many years before. A safehouse, but maybe also a place with answers, to shed some light on the situation here, on the secrets Selina had come to unearth.

SAGE

"Of all my past lives, I'm most proud of a particular one that lasted only twenty-seven years," Hiro said.

This after an extended silence, Sage half-napping to recover a bit of energy before they touched down in Rhodes. They looked up at Hiro, raised an eyebrow at him. Evidently he took this as encouragement.

"I lived most of my life in a Buddhist monastery in the latter half of the 14th century. We practiced Jōdo Shinshū Buddhism, which taught that all are equal. In Japan, the peasants had been heavily oppressed for centuries. In the last two years of my life I took up arms and fought alongside peasants and a few Shinto priests to free the people from the tyranny of our samurai overlords."

Hiro paused and seemed to watch Sage. "I took an arrow in combat, and was captured. The next day they executed me. Our rebellion failed horribly, and it would be many more centuries before all of the Japanese people were able to live in relative freedom. Nonetheless, it brings me great pride to remember the battles we fought and won, even though we ultimately lost."

"Why are you telling me this?" Sage asked.

"Now it's your turn," Hiro said, smiling.

"I didn't have any past lives, sorry," Sage said.

"Of course you do. Like most, you've simply not received the training necessary to remember them. But never mind that. I thought you might just share something about your past with me, something to help me get to know you better."

"I see what you're doing," Sage said, shifting uncomfortably in their chair to look at Hiro, his smiling eyes and ridiculous tie. "You're fishing to find out what biological sex I was before. My partners always do this, like my sexual chromosomes define the person I am and was always meant to be."

Hiro's eyes never stopped smiling, but he held his arms up in conciliation. "I don't care about all of that. Do you think that in all of my lives I was a man?"

Sage looked at Hiro for a long time, digesting this nugget. He seemed sincere, and if he was crazy at least he had proven that he had their back. "What did you want to know then?"

Hiro produced a small can of tea from his bag and cracked it open. He offered them the can, taking a sip himself after they refused. "Something good about your past. We're partners. Partners in vigilante justice at this point. We ought to know each other, don't you think?"

"Fine," Sage said. "I'll tell you what I meant when I told that punk kid I was always thinking with my bits."

Hiro nodded, and waited.

"When I was thirteen there was an older boy I met in a café in Rome. I could tell he was bad news – I've always had a great sense for that sort of thing – but he seduced me and I went back to his place anyway. He was probably three or four years older than I was, and overpowered me with ease when we got there. He took my wallet and raped me, then kicked me back out onto the street."

"Wow," Hiro said. "I had no idea. No wonder...."

"No wonder I had the surgery?"

Hiro shrugged, clearly sensing he'd miss-stepped.

Sage leaned in. "Understand this, partner of mine. My choice to have the surgery has nothing to do with the fact that some boy made me a victim long ago. I chose to become this way biologically because I was always this way mentally. Sexual impulse has always been an obstacle to self-betterment. My interests were never in sex or partnering up with someone else, but in history, science, combat. Justice. And my choice transformed me not just into an 'andro,' as people say, but into a better person. A better agent."

Hiro grinned, and gave a surprisingly convincing bow for someone sitting in a shuttle seat. "Thank you, Sage," he said. "I believe I know you much better now than before."

"You're welcome, I suppose," Sage said. And then, after a moment, they reached out for Hiroyuki's can of tea, and grabbed it. Took a modest drink, and returned it. It tasted smooth, but with a hint of something grassy, a hint of something bitter. Sage had not really ever been a tea person, but this wasn't so bad.

"Buckle up," came the voice from the PA system. "We're inbound to Rhodes and will be landing momentarily."

Sage buckled up and waited.

GASH

"The best thing about this island is that it's dry. I can smoke here," Gash said to nobody in particular, lighting up a cigarette and gulping the smoke into his lungs. They stood before a building that gave true meaning to the word "ruins." It had been set into the hillside centuries ago, but now very little of the structure remained. Gash could see what had once been architectural features. That these were manmade could only be determined because they had unnatural shapes (circular or rectangular).

"Oh yes, this is a much nicer place to stay than that hotel," Frederick said, lugging his and Selina's suitcases from the Jeep towards the crumbling monastery.

"You're from Detroit, right?" Gash asked.

"Yes," Frederick said

"So you should feel right at home living in a ruined building," Gash laughed, short and harsh.

Frederick rolled his eyes and Selina shot him a look. He puffed in on his cigarette and blew a cloud of smoke at her face.

"What a reticent employee I'm stuck with," Selina said, giving him a soft shove to the shoulder.

Gash led the way in, stepping over rubble and kicking up dust as he did. The walls had been carved into the hillside, and it became clear that they were entering what essentially amounted to a cave in the hills of Rhodes. Debris and dirt littered the path, and the group passed by several side passages that had caved in long ago. When it grew dark in the absence of the sun's natural light, Selina powered on a mobile lantern she'd packed away with her other things.

Eventually, Gash led them into a large open space, what Selina and Frederick agreed had probably been used as a mess hall. Old stone benches lined the hall, pulled up before what once were wooden tables. Several side passages stood open from there, and the group stopped. Frederick set down the bags, and Gash dropped his own duffle bag.

"We should split up and make sure it's safe. Right?" Selina turned to Gash for confirmation.

"Nah," Gash said, dropped his cigarette butt to the floor and grinding it out. "You two should set up shop here, and I'll scope out the side passages, make sure it's safe. That's my job, after all. And I want to be a good employee." He raised an eyebrow at Selina, who looked away to conceal a small smile.

When she looked up, it was to toss him a second LED lantern. He grabbed it, chose the nearest passage, and started walking, his hand never far from the magnum. The place seemed quiet enough, and Gash hadn't gotten any kind of vibe from the hotel owner that he was sending them into a trap, but still it always paid to be careful.

Gash didn't like how his footsteps echoed this deep in the monastery. He didn't like how empty it was, and he didn't like that nothing was going on. If things weren't happening, his mind wandered. Last time, it brought him a heaping pile of Lulu-related guilt. This time, it wound its way back to Serena. She'd always wanted to travel, but they'd never quite had the money or the time. He'd told her stories about places he'd been in the service, and she'd always sighed and looked off into the distance, obviously romanticizing. Now here he was again, in a dangerous foreign place, somewhere drab and hot with death around each corner, and Serena would have longed to join him, would have imagined a Mediterranean beach destination and pined for it when he told the story. Only Serena was dead, of course, and Gash would never be able to tell her this story, or any other.

The day she died, Serena had been so sure of herself. So full of joy to have finally found a way to climb out of her addiction. They had talked for hours that morning, Serena crying about all the pain her addiction had brought him. Had brought her. They had laughed, too, and curled into each other's naked selves. It had been one of the only pleasant spring days that year, a flash of time between the harsh cold of winter and the blistering heat of summer. Through the open window the curtains danced in the breeze, the same breeze that tickled the hairs on his thighs and arms. Gash had splurged on synth-bacon – the good kind, too, imported from the clinics in Osaka, and between the two of them they'd finished off the whole pack.

Gash clenched his fist, longing for something to connect it to, someone bad on which he could vent his rage. But he found no one, only a dusty corridor that wound through the hill, small empty rooms that had once been prayer rooms or residences or who-knew-what.

He reached the end, a cave-in that blocked his progress, and began to return to the central hall. He covered about a third of the distance back before he heard Frederick shouting, shrill with fear.

Shit. Shit. They split up twice in two days, and danger came charging in both times. And now he'd failed her again, Serena – no, Selina – and she would be killed and Gash would continue to walk the Earth alone, a death curse to those who knew him, a man who could never know respite.

SAGE

"I have a bad feeling," Hiroyuki said.

Sage looked out the window. The shuttle was descending towards a small tarmac on the other end of the island from the main city. The setting sun cast waves of red light from the western horizon, shimmering crimson in the thick atmosphere. There were two vehicles parked on the edge of the tiny shuttleport, and they saw figures emerging from those vehicles. At least half a dozen, maybe more. The shuttle banked, and Sage could no longer see directly down.

"Looks like you're right, partner," Sage said. "I believe our pilot friend has taken our money and set us up."

Hiro's eyes glimmered. "If you can't trust a bribed corporate mercenary, who *can* you trust?"

"Fair point. Should have expected something like this."

"Want to go take out the pilot?" Hiro asked.

Sage shook their head. "Those doors are made from a carbon nanotube shell. We couldn't get in there without blowing the whole shuttle. Plus, even if we did, can you fly one of these things?"

Hiro finished a last swig from his can of tea, and shook his head. "Me neither."

"What's the plan, then?"

Sage unbuckled themself and pulled down their goodie bag from the storage space above the seats. Placed it on their seat, between them and Hiro, opened it up. Inside were Sage's two favorite gauss pistols, and a variety of other goodies. They took stock of the hardware with Hiro, and the two of them made a plan.

Moments later, as the shuttle made contact with hard earth, Sage dropped a smoke grenade to the floor of the cabin. It exploded with a hiss. When the back of the shuttle opened up and the ramp descended to the tarmac, a half dozen Knights in long red overcoats were met with a cloud of billowing smoke.

At the same time, a small charge on the far side of the shuttle detonated with a soft click and then a loud boom. Sage dove out the fresh hole in the side of the shuttle, and hit the ground hard, rolling to compensate. They could feel tiny pieces of gravel digging into the flesh of their right shoulder. A warm trickle of blood as Sage rolled to their feet and drew their gauss pistols just in time for one of the Knights to poke his head around the side of the shuttle to see what was going on.

Sage fired both weapons at once, the hail of metal flechettes shredding the would-be attacker before he could get a shot off from the antique submachine gun he was toting.

The element of surprise had gone in Sage's favor so far. But there wasn't cover here, they had to get around to the nose of the shuttle. They scrambled across the tarmac, ducking around the nose of the craft just as another Knight popped out from the tail end to fire a steady stream of bullets at them. They raked the pavement, kicking up black dust at Sage's feet.

They looked up at the cockpit, but it was too high to get a good look, and the windows were heavily tinted. Sage resisted the urge to fire up at the cockpit, that backstabbing pilot. The plan was to split the Knights apart, so Hiroyuki could take half and Sage could take half. If they got distracted with the pilot, then Hiro would certainly be overwhelmed.

The SMG fire continued to come, and Sage was counting on the fact that at least one other Hospitaller would be trying to flank them around the other end of the shuttle. They counted to three, eyes closed, and then rolled out from behind cover on the opposite end of the shuttle. Sure enough, the Knight clutching a shotgun in both hands had just enough time to register her surprise and call out in dismay before catching two in the chest from Sage's gauss weapons and being thrown backwards half the length of the shuttle.

Sage darted back behind the plane and immediately sprinted out the other end. The Knight that had been laying down covering fire, trying to distract them from the flanking maneuver, had shifted sides to where Sage had taken down his fellow Knight. Sage ran hard at an angle from the shuttle. Only had a few seconds to get a good angle on the third and final Knight before he figured out which side they was coming at him from. Hopefully Hiro was winning his fight as well. Sage heard the sound of gunfire from within the plane, sporadic and frantic.

When Sage came around the back of the shuttle at a distance, their assailant was prepared, having taken cover on the far side of the vessel. He was smarter than they'd given him credit for. He opened fire, ricochets from the tarmac flicking gravel stingers at Sage's ankles. This hadn't quite gone according to plan, but the Knights' inexplicable preference for gunpowder weapons would still give Sage an edge. Gauss weapons were more accurate, and packed a bigger punch. Still sprinting as fast as they could to make it harder for the Hospitaller to track them, Sage drew a bead and fired back. Emptied both clips. Magnetized metal flechettes at super-sonic speeds punched through the hull of the shuttle and into the Knight. He fell over backwards, blood pooling on the tarmac.

Inside the shuttle, gunfire had ceased. Sage reloaded and entered, the smoke beginning to clear, drifting through the openings and dispersing in the dusk air. Hiro stood facing them, hands behind his back, smiling placidly. The other three Knights were all dead, strewn about the interior of the shuttlecraft, limbs and necks at awkward, painful angles.

"I don't suppose we got one of them alive?" Sage asked.

Without answering, Hiro turned and took three steps to the cockpit door. He was still in stride when it opened, the pilot evidently coming out to collect some kind of bounty from the Knights. Hiro grabbed his hand, and smoothly pulled him out, propelling him into the waiting arms of Sage, who was not so gentle with the back-stabber. They swept him to the shuttle floor, his head cracking. When he looked to the left, he found himself parallel to the rolled back eyes of one of the dead Knights.

You didn't need Sage's special gift for reading people's emotions to see the terror plain on the pilot's face.

"My partner needs a reason not to choke the life out of you," Hiro said calmly. "They has some rage issues I think."

"We paid you an awful lot only to be delivered into an ambush," Sage added, their fingers tightening slowly around the pilot's throat.

"I'm sorry," the pilot gasped. "The first time I flew Gerard to Rhodes was five years ago. He and a few others of his people took me to some old ruins, like a temple in a cave, and made me watch while they executed these three men. They used a fucking antique to cut their heads off. I think he called it a guillotine. It was a horror show. I couldn't betray them, I don't want to die like that."

"The Knights have a *guillotine*?" Sage asked.

"From the reading you've given me, it does seem that they have a penchant for old fashioned methods of destruction," Hiro said.

"Where is this Hospitaller base with the guillotine?" Sage asked.

"I'll show you on a map, I remember it really well." He swallowed with great difficult around the vise-grip Sage had on his throat. "I'll certainly never forget that day."

"Good," Sage said. "You'll show me, and then you'll see to it that repairing the hull of your shuttle takes exactly as long as it takes my partner and I to take care of business and return for you. If I don't have a return ride to Paris waiting for me when I get back here, I'll hunt you to the ends of the Earth, and you'll *wish* I'd only used a guillotine when I'm done with you. Clear?"

"Crystal," the pilot said.

SELINA

They'd come from nowhere, men and women in white robes with wide thin swords. Selina had barely fallen out of the way of a pair of thrown knives that had grazed her cheek, drawing thin beads of blood from within, pooling and dripping down her chin even as she staggered to her feet and Frederick shouted in surprise.

There must have been at least a dozen of the robed figures, and the eyes set into bald heads seemed empty of life, or at least of emotion. They moved with the precision of automatons, and Selina almost fancied for a moment that they were. But of course that sort of tech was still decades away.

She produced her weapon, still on lethal mode from before, and fired off a couple of shots. One of the attackers went down, and the rest took cover behind some tables. They shifted in both directions, trying to flank her and Frederick.

He grabbed her other hand and pulled. "We have to get into a better position," he said.

They backed up, Selina firing at anyone who broke cover, into one of the other corridors. Assuming nothing had been hiding in here when they arrived, at least Selina and Frederick would be protected from the sides. But the attackers would quickly overwhelm them. And Gash was coming. Would he be ambushed and killed while they took shelter here, holding back these robed figures?

She still had Mauricio's old pistol in her shoulder bag. She pulled it out and tossed it to Frederick. "Know how to use one of these?"

"Detroit," he said. "Remember?"

The two of them unleashed a volley on the attackers, dropping another. The robed figures moved in perfect unison, gathering stone benches into a semicircle, and stacking them on top of each other to provide cover. And they waited. Gash. They must have known he was there, or maybe heard his footsteps coming back. They were going to take him out and then take their time with Selina and Frederick.

Strange that they had swords and knives, but no guns. These were not the Knights, who favored augmentations and firearms and blood-red cloaks. Which left the Order of the White Lotus that the hotel proprietor had spoken of. Apparently, the enemy of their enemy was not their friend. Another pair of throwing knives landed inches from her head, buried deep in the stone wall. Selina returned fire.

And she saw Gash come crashing out of the corridor. He gave an inhuman roar and, without slowing down, charged headlong into the remaining ten attackers, firing his hand cannon. Two dropped at once, apparently unprepared for the ferocity of his onslaught. But they recovered quickly, swarming him on all sides, swords flashing. He ducked under a horizontal slash from the nearest, rammed his gun into her belly, and fired once. Before she could slump to the floor, he was on to the next, deflecting a sword stroke with the long barrel of the magnum, and bringing it back around, the explosion of gunpowder throwing the assailant's head back into the wall with a violent crack.

The gun spent, Gash hurled it at a charging swordsman, taking the half second he'd bought himself to crouch down and draw a long knife from his own boot. When he rose again, it was beneath the downstroke of a sword blade to bury his knife in his attacker's belly.

Selina stood in stunned awe. This wasn't a washed out P.I. fighting, this was a commando. Some kind of super soldier. A human man possessed by a demon. He flowed around attacks from trained swordsmen like water, swinging his knife, blood arcing into the air. Selina could only watch the dance, almost beautiful, Gash felling their attackers one at a time. Until he stumbled sideways, a throwing knife in his side.

There were only three of the robed figures left, and they prepared to descend on their wounded prey, Selina and Frederick forgotten in the frenzy. The two emerged from the corridor firing, and quickly dropped the final three White Lotus before they could finish Gash off. He took a couple of steps towards her grinning. "You're still alive," he muttered, before collapsing to the hard stone floor.

GASH

With great difficulty Gash forced his eyes open. The light of a nearby lantern flared, a supernova to his retinas; he blinked rapidly. His side throbbed. He took stock of his surroundings.

Selina and Frederick had managed to drag him onto a sleeping pad, and set up a mobile med unit. It currently read his pulse from a few feet away, beeping gently in tune with the thumping of his heart.

"Nothing vital," Selina said, leaning in from the other side until her hair brushed lightly against his bare chest. He checked the bandage around his chest.

"This is a pretty good job. You have some kind of medical training?"

Selina looked down at him. "No, but you live the kind of life I do, you learn a variety of skills."

He reached up and put his hand on her face.

Her head snapped back, and she brushed the hand away.

"Thank you," he said softly, his hand returning to his side. "For patching me up."

"Thank you too," she said fiercely, "for saving us. But after what

I just saw, I think you have some explaining to do."

Gash propped himself up on his elbows. His side burned like crazy, but the pain gave him clarity. Plus he could already feel that the medigel Selina had applied to the wound was bonding it shut. He should be good to walk in an hour or so, though it would be weeks before he was back to full strength. Frederick sat at a distance, taking a back seat to Selina and Gash's discussion, as usual. But something burned in his eyes. Something hard. It disappeared quickly, leaving Gash to wonder if he'd imagined it. The kid was from Detroit, but all joking about one of America's most downtrodden cities aside, had always seemed mostly harmless.

"Who are you," Selina pressed. "You told me you were a down-and-out private investigator from Seattle, on the run from WalCo for reasons unnamed. But you single-handedly attacked ten trained, sword-wielding assassins with a pistol and a knife at close quarters, and almost won. Has anything you've told me yet been true?"

"All of it," Gash said, the dryness in his throat gumming up the words. Selina brought a small canteen of water to his lips. She *was* prepared. He sipped enough to clear his throat. "Thanks," he said.

She put the canteen away and looked expectantly at him.

"If I've lied to you, it's been by omission. Being my employer doesn't entitle you to my life story," he said. She was about to speak, but he held his hand up to silence her. "*But.* It does entitle you to know that I wasn't always a P.I. Before that, I was in the service. Spec ops in the military, and then when that shut down I worked for the Marine Corporation awhile. There were experiments using adrenal and hormonal shots to augment reflexes and strength and aim. I honestly don't know if that stuff made a difference. There's always been a darkness inside me that excels at killing. That thrives on it. I try not to unleash it, but I do when it's needed."

"Did you get some kind of augs?"

Gash reached into the pocket of his jacket, on the ground beside him. Fished out a cigarette and lighter. Fired up one of the smokes and took a deep drag. "You can turn any asshole into a super soldier if you replace his natural parts with artificial parts. But the idea of my program was to enhance what already existed. I haven't heard much since I left the program, so I think it was probably a failure."

"You're talking about a super soldier serum," Selina said, laughing. "That's some comic book shit, right there."

Gash shrugged, then just as quickly regretted it as a sharp spike of pain pulsated out from his wound and racked his body. He laid back down.

"While we're talking comic book shit," Selina continued, "one of the assassins had a pamphlet of sorts in his robes. Some kind of manifesto. My PCom translated for me, and get this – it's written in Cantonese."

"A dead language," Gash said, eyebrows raised.

"Still used in the Chinese underworld," Frederick chimed in. When both Gash and Selina looked at him he looked away. "I looked it up once," he said.

"What's it say?" Gash asked.

"It's talking about magic," Selina said. "About how the West blocked magic from the world. Mostly it lists all the terrible things that have happened to the world since that happened. The loss of rituals to ward off evil spirits and possession. The loss of efficacy of healing methods like acupuncture meant to channel chi. Climate change, apparently?" Selina laughed. "It's a trippy read."

"Magic?" Gash said. "What the hell would they want on a little island off the coast of Turkey then?"

"Haven't got a clue."

"Are you sure you translated it correctly?"

"I paid quite a lot for this translation software, and it comes highly recommended. Yes, I'm sure."

"Guys," Frederick said. "I know it sounds a little crazy, but think about it. Every mythology in the world references the supernatural. Ghosts, sorcerers, witches."

"The tooth fairy," Gash chimed in.

Selina giggled and Frederick looked away.

"Oh come on," Selina said, squeezing Frederick's arm. "Magic? Don't be silly."

"Okay, fine," he said.

Selina rose to her feet. "Anyway, I'm glad you're okay, Gash. It's good to have a super-soldier on my team."

"I'm not a –"

"I'm kidding. Mostly." She stepped back, and grabbed Gash's magnum off a bench, handed it to him. "I loaded it for you. Sit tight, and if any more assassins show up, dust 'them."

"Where do you think you're going?" he asked.

"I'm going to finish scoping out the ruins. Do a little archaeologisting."

"That's not a word," Frederick chimed in helpfully. "But I'm here to help."

"No, for now stay here and protect Gash for me. There should be more ammo for the pistol I gave you in the bag over there. I stocked up before we left, just in case."

"I don't need to be protected," Gash growled.

"Fine," Selina said, looking from Gash to Frederick and back again. "Frederick, stay behind and protect our camp. If more assassins show up, let them kill Gash, but don't let them take any of our stuff."

Gash watched her walk into the darkness of a nearby passage, the light of her portable lantern a halo around her back, the soft patter of her steps echoing in moderate staccato but growing distant as the light grew smaller, until she turned around a corner and the passageway grew dark again.

He took a look at his magnum. The metal of the barrel had been chipped by a sword stroke, but fortunately nothing that would impair the gun's ability to function. He'd have to be more careful with his weapon; there would be, he suspected, plenty of need for it before he was done with the Isle of Rhodes.

SELINA

It took Selina something like three hours to discover anything of significance in the temple, which proved predominantly to be empty corridors and long-decayed furniture. The place had been cleaned out long ago. When she did finally discover something of note, what she found left her breathless.

The room was larger than the others, and someone had taken time to overlay mahogany paneling – real, as far as Selina could tell – over the raw stone walls.

Within stood a guillotine that had obviously been destroyed intentionally, the blade on the floor beside collapsed wood, the bloodstains on the floor beneath it old, but not old enough. Selina had little time to be disturbed by the prospect, for behind it, on a large stone pedestal, stood a foot. A foot as large as Selina, carved from stone and coated by a thin plate of bronze turned black by time and the forces of oxidization. The foot had been cleanly severed at the ankle, the interior stone showing signs of scorching, the bronze near the break clearly having been liquefied in extreme heat before cooling off and re-solidifying.

A piece of the Colossus of Rhodes. Almost exactly as Rembert had described it in the little journal her father had given her as a child. Not carried away by the Ottomans centuries ago, as the histories suggested. Not broken off at the knee because of an earthquake, as the histories suggested. Something had taken it off cleanly. What? It looked like the work of a high-powered laser, but of course such technology was only now just barely coming into use.

Selina reeled with the implications, each at war with each other. Did this mean that Rhodes was visited by ancient aliens? That seemed improbable. Could natural forces be responsible for something like this, somehow? Selina did not have time to consult an expert, but this, too, seemed unlikely. Perhaps the fanciful talk of magic in the White Lotus pamphlet would turn out not to be so fanciful after all. Bubbling beneath the surface of all of Selina's questions were more practical matters. Why would the Knights keep something like this a secret for over a thousand years? What would it mean for Selina to have discovered it for the world of non-secret organizations? Certainly fame and fortune would follow such a thing.

Smart money would be on calling in a team of prospectors and mercs from the Florida University Board. As an expedition funded by Florida State U., Selina's little group had the right to call for backup and still claim primary credit for the discovery. The school would get to display the Colossus Foot, but Selina would be known, well-paid. Could finally move on, pursue her Mayan lineage, and see what could be dug up in the Yucatan Peninsula. This little journal, the Colossus, had only been a means to an end. And here was the means.

But something clawed at her, inside. These new discoveries had eclipsed her childhood obsession. Getting credit for finding the Colossus now took a back seat to unravelling the mystery of the Pit, to finding the connection between that and whatever mysterious forces originally brought down the great statue. More than anything, Selina needed answers. There was a hole in Rhodes, and a secret Chinese organization that seemed to believe that magic was real. If she called in an army, there would be devastation. A war, as the Knights and the

White Lotus and the mercs all battled. Things would be destroyed, the truth could be lost.

So what would be the next step? The hotel clerk had accidentally sent them to a former secret Hospitaller base. The guillotine had been vandalized, and it hadn't been Knights that had come to kill them when they arrived. So the White Lotus had pushed the Knights out of the countryside, forcing them to abandon their base. And Selina had stumbled upon their secret – what, trophy room? Execution room? – in the dark heart of the old abandoned temple.

Trying to connect all the dots in her head was proving difficult. She closed her eyes and tried to force everything out, so that she could invite the facts in one at a time and consider them all in due course. A strategy she'd learned for coping with the death of her parents, and used from time to time when the world became overwhelming. Only no sooner had she started, but she heard voices raised echoing down the halls from where she'd left Gash and Frederick. No gunshots yet, but that didn't mean much.

Stun gun in hand and lethal mode engaged, Selina rushed down the corridor. When she appeared, it was to join a standoff between her team and two others. Gash and Frederick both had weapons pointed at an individual wearing a loose blue shirt and khaki pants, a wicked-looking gauss pistol in each hand. Lithe and well-muscled with short blonde hair and a weathered face that seemed to be permanently set into a scowl, this angry gunslinger had a weapon pointed at both of Selina's people. Behind, almost an after-thought, stood an apparently unarmed Japanese man in business casual, with an orange tie that proved, upon closer inspection, to be the likeness of an upside down Buddha. His demeanor seemed so placid that Selina almost forgot about the impending gunfight.

Almost.

She leveled her stun gun at the gunslinger. "Whatever's happening right now, you have about six seconds to put those weapons away."

"That's what I've been telling your friends," the gunslinger said, voice a steel filament. "You go first, and I'll follow suit."

SAGE

The two men were not who Sage had expected to find when they arrived at the Hospitaller base. One of them, long and grizzled, had been stretched out on a sleeping pad, a bandage around his chest. His pale skin, gaunt face, and unkempt dark hair gave him the appearance of one near death's door. Sage saw a darkness in him, but did not think Hospitaller. The other was younger, but Sage found it impossible to say by how much. He was Aryan – blonde hair and blue eyes. Sage saw a softness in him that seemed almost an affectation. Very strange. But when Sage looked past these two, all of that was forgotten. They heard Hiro's breath catch when he saw it too.

The place looked like a slaughterhouse. A dozen bodies had been scattered, limbs askew and blood everywhere, around a makeshift barricade of stone benches. White-robed men and women of predominantly Chinese, Japanese, and Korean descent. Like all the other victims of Gerard and his people. These had to be Hospitallers.

When Sage and Hiro had been detected, both men were quick to point old firearms and shout threats. Sage had returned the favor, their gauss weapons having already been drawn before they entered with Hiro. For his part, Hiro, seemed unperturbed by the sudden hostilities.

When they looked up from the standoff and saw the girl approaching with her stun gun, diminutive but somehow powerful, burnished skin smooth with the newness of youth but brown eyes burning with something much older, Sage's gut made it clear that these were not Hospitallers.

But they found it hard to trust their gut when confronted with the overwhelming evidence. What were they doing in a Hospitaller base? The two exchanged hostilities, but then Hiro quietly pressed down on Sage's weapons until they rested at their side. The odd group of three lowered weapons as well at this, vindicating Sage's intuition.

"Who the hell are you?" said the young woman.

"I could ask the same," Sage retorted. "And complete the package with 'what the hell are you doing here?'"

Hiro stepped past Sage and bowed to them. "Forgive my partner here, they tends naturally to be suspicious, and we were led to believe we would find something different at this location."

"What, different from three armed strangers and a pile of white-robed bodies?" the wounded man quipped.

"Look," Sage said. "We're chasing a dangerous band of criminals, and this looks like their handiwork. It's not safe here, and I need you three to debrief me on what you know, and then get to safety."

"From your demeanor and your Italian accent, I'd peg you for Interpol," the injured man said. "But you're dressed like tourists."

"We're on special assignment," Sage said.

The group of three exchanged glances, and then the young woman spoke. "My name is Selina. My companions are Gash and Frederick. You should know that this bloodbath is our handiwork, but also that it was self-defense. I'll fill you in on what we've encountered since arriving on Rhodes, but you're going to have to do the same. I know of Interpol, but I don't for a second believe you're here on anything sanctioned by your organization. There would be more of you if you were. A lot more."

Selina

The Interpol agent's name had turned out to be Sage, and their partner's to be Hiroyuki. They were pursuing the Hospitallers on their own. Sage had been chasing that organization for years. When Selina had let them know of the multiple attacks, filled them in on the White Lotus as well, the look of incredulity on Sage's face had been striking. It was a bizarre conspiracy story that Selina wove for the Interpol agents, but, as soon became evident, Selina was only confirming the bizarre conspiracy theory Sage had been wrestling with for years, unable to prove the existence of an organization that seemed fantastical in nature.

When it became clear to Sage that the Hospitallers had a central base on the island, that was the end of the conversation. They insisted that the group take them there. But Selina was loathe to force Gash into motion just yet, and not quite yet finished with the discovery of this lone piece of the Colossus. What else would this old temple hold within?

Frederick had not been keen to guide Sage. But it was needed. If they could put Interpol in front of the Hospitallers, then they would only have to get through whatever White Lotus remained to unravel the full mystery of the island. What happened to the Colossus? Why was everyone talking about magic? And why was there a hole in the Earth beneath the island?

"Keep your head down, stay in public, don't draw attention," Selina had told him. "We'll meet at the Pit in a few hours and see if we can figure out how to excavate the site."

He had dutifully agreed, admitting it would be nice to have the Knights off their trail. Perhaps Interpol would go after the White Lotus next; they'd been implicated in plenty of killings as well.

When the three were gone, Selina found herself alone with Gash for the first time since they'd left for Rhodes. She remembered earlier that night when Gash had touched her face. The warmth that had lanced through her. Why? Where had it come from? He certainly proved to be an imposing fighter. But his face left something to be desired, and he was much older than she was. Not her type at all.

Still, something appealed. Clearly this man had been broken and reforged many times over by the world, but remained, in a particular way, fractured. When the dim afterglow of Sage's flashlight vanished from the far recesses of the hallway towards the exit, she locked eyes with Gash. And before she knew what was happening, Selina found herself leaning in to kiss the grizzled ex-P.I. It was clear he wanted her, and it had been a very long time since Selina had enjoyed herself. He hesitated for a moment – unsure of her intent or perhaps of whether this was a good idea – and then put his hand on her face again and their lips met.

They kissed. He tasted of cigarette smoke and used too much tongue. Selina was reaching for his belt when her PCom buzzed. Gash laughed and she leaned back, exhaling, and flicked the button to answer the inbound call, which turned out to be from Hemmingway. He was calling virtually, so when the holodisplay answered the call, it projected a 3-D version of his avatar's face. She'd still never met the real Hemmingway.

"Starfire, Gash, good. You're both there. This is important, so listen up."

"Hi to you, too, Hemmingway," Selina said. "None of the usual pleasantries?"

"You know I have a pretty extensive network of contacts, yes?"

Selina looked at Gash, his face masked, and then expectantly back at Hemmingway.

"Well there's trouble headed your way, of the big variety," he continued.

"Out with it, then," Gash said.

"Oh I'm sorry, am I interrupting something with my tedious attempt to save your lives for free?" Hemmingway said.

"We're sorry," Selina said. "Could you please tell us what's going on?"

In the background of the call, Hemmingway's pornographic maid flicked diminutively at his shoulders with her feather duster. He shooed her, and she fluttered away, exasperation written ostentatiously across her face.

"It's WalCo, somehow they found out that you hacked them. AND they know you're with Gash. I don't know how they figured that all out," he trailed off.

"They're WalCo," Gash said. "What they spend on surveillance? I'd be surprised if they didn't know."

"Well I've been helping Starfire cover her tracks, and usually that's good enough. Whatever you stole, girl, must've been heavy stuff."

"Why? What are they doing?" she said.

"They have an off-books facility in central Washington, on the fringe of the Seattle sprawl. About two hours ago they launched a troop transport, and its destination is confirmed as Rhodes."

The silence expanded from that statement, filling the room with soft nothing. Eventually Selina sighed. "Thanks for the tip, but we've handled a lot already. I think we're more than capable of –"

"No," Gash cut her off. "We're not. Trust me. We need to get off this island immediately. A secret organization of sword fighting warrior monks and another secret organization with roots in a knightly monastic order? That sucks, and it's badass that we've been able to take them on without dying. But what Hemmingway is talking about is a corporate black-ops team of at least ten highly trained operatives. Each of them heavily cybered and armed with enough firepower to wipe out every single human being on this island, if that's what WalCo called for. We *cannot* handle this."

"He's right," Hemmingway added.

Selina sat back. So that was it, then. Cut and run. They were right, of course. Even with two Interpol agents on their side, they couldn't handle that sort of firepower. And Selina couldn't call in mercs, not now. The FUB would turn their men right around the instant they found out that WalCo was coming down on Rhodes.

It was run or die time. But Selina wouldn't run. The more she thought about it, the more the thought took root deep within her. Nothing would move her from this path. Her life's work, her ticket out of the slums of Jacksonville, her father's dying wish. Not even WalCo could shake her loose from this.

"Hemmingway, I'm going to need your help running an op."

"Starfire, please tell me you're kidding. You're going to hack WalCo's black ops division using a PCom and the ambient Wi-Fi in middle-of-nowhere Rhodes? You won't have the bandwidth to feel *anything*."

"I'll pay, if you want. I'm hoping they haven't found that backdoor you set me up with for the first op. If they have, I'm probably screwed. But it doesn't matter. No chance is WalCo going to chase me off this island until I have the answers I need."

Gash laughed. Hemmingway and Selina both looked at him. "What? I'm just impressed. She's got more backbone than most of the professional soldiers I served with."

"Well, can you at least do it without jacking in? I don't want you getting fried if they catch you."

It was Selina's turn to laugh. "Hack them *without* jacking in? I couldn't do that with my rig at home and a month to plan it, you know this."

"You're right." Hemmingway paused. "This is a terrible idea, Starfire."

"But you'll help, won't you?"

"I will. We can discuss my fee if you survive the op, whatever craziness is going on in Rhodes, and your trip back here to Florida."

"Thanks, Hemmingway. Here's what I'm going to need from you."

STARFIRE

Starfire relished the rush of jacking in, the torrent of stars flooding her vision, a cloned version of her home rig's OS that she'd programmed for her PCom neural interface. She wasted no time – there was none to waste, and she didn't want to give herself time to get cold feet. She turned and flew towards a nearby star, and before long found herself diving through a series of disused network nodes. She flew too fast to stop and see the sites. An amalgamation of memory and feeling took her through the dummy sites, each of them another step that WalCo OpSec would have to take to trace things back to her. Two dozen of these, and she slowed. She selected with minimal review from a database of unprotected business startups and never-made-it-big social media nodes that Hemmingway had probably just pulled from the Shodan search engine, and blasted through these as well. A few had skinned their private nodes for the aesthetics of their programmers and users. Starfire flew through a small Japanese town, a poorly coded Roman bath house, and three mock-libraries.

After two dozen dummy nodes and half as many from

Hemmingway's list of unsecureds, Starfire pulled up. It was time to go for the backdoor.

"I'm in position. Do you have a lock yet?"

"Damn, Stars, you work fast."

"Is that my new nickname?"

"Yeah, do you like it?"

"Only if I can call you Hemmy," she said.

A short laugh. "Okay, Starfire. Yes, I do have a lock. Transferring to your PCom now."

With a thought, she called the new feed up. In the corner of her vision, Starfire could see a grainy satellite image, tracking a small black dot across the Atlantic Ocean. Displayed beneath the image, a constantly changing string of forty numbers representing the transport's latitude and longitude.

"Can this be traced back to you?" Starfire asked.

"Thanks for thinking of me, but don't worry. This is an old imaging satellite. Hasn't been used in a decade, and when you're done, I'm poised to remotely fry the thing's motherboard. No chance they'll trace it to me."

"Good, then get out. I'll let you know when it's done. If you haven't heard from me in an hour, assume I got fried."

From the silence, she assumed Hemmingway was gone. This was it, the moment of truth.

There would be no time for finesse, and they already wanted to kill her, so there was no point trying to avoid detection. No point trying to avoid attribution. She hit the backdoor at full speed, and blasted through. It was still there, that was a great start.

WalCo nodes were all skinned in Matrix theme. Too serious for aesthetically pleasing skins, major corporations nevertheless needed to take full advantage of the benefits of neural immersion for the purposes of coding. Matrix theme, named for the science fiction movie from the late Twentieth Century, used three-dimensionally stacked sheets of coding – encrypted of course – to represent their digital interests. The outcome to a coder, or in this case to a black hat like Selina, was dramatic in its own right. Selina floated at "ground level" in a veritable metropolis of code. Thin lines of streaming green characters stacked up and up, beyond the scope of what Selina could see with her PCom's rudimentary processing speed. Each skyscraper's worth of data corresponded to a major database or facility. All of it linked, from WalCo's Seattle HQ to its Berlin office, to rivers of "underground" data representing the unsanctioned research with which a mega-corporation like WalCo was doubtless engaged. She'd dipped her digital fingers into one such river the last time she was here, without knowing what she was stealing or to whom Mauricio was handing off the data.

Last time, there had been thousands of bright lights, like willow-wisps floating in the stacks. Each of them represented a coder, or a white hat testing WalCo security parameters. The digital residents of the neural network. To them, she knew, she would be simply one more green point of light. Acknowledged as authorized by the system by virtue of her backdoor access. She wouldn't hold up to intense scrutiny, but with so many ostensibly authorized users working the stacks at once, nobody could scrutinize each one. Nor would they try, when automated systems were supposedly in place to make such "authorized" access by an outsider impossible.

No such lights were visible now. The stacks shone and shimmered with hourly changes to encryption keys, but not one wisp flickered between data streams. Not one user. It was night in Seattle, but WalCo had offices in Europe, Asia, Australia, Africa, and probably everywhere else in the world. Hell, the network even extended on tight-wave laser broadband to Lunar City. Was this routine maintenance, then? Everyone out while WalCo updated the systems? Unlikely, but possible. What else could it be? Did they know she was coming, was this an ambush? Every impulse in Starfire screamed retreat. But there couldn't be retreat. Now that she'd started down this path, she'd burned all the time they would have needed to escape before the WalCo black ops team landed.

Onward. Her tools were limited – she had pulled what she could from her home network before starting this op, but with her PCom's marginal processing power, much of what she'd written was out of play. Still, Starfire was known in the community for innovation. She ran a cloaking program first. If this was some routine maintenance, she would no longer appear as a point of light to other users. If they were actively looking for her, on the other hand, this would barely slow them down. But it was a start. She kept several bots ready to deploy, depending on what came next.

For a moment, there was nothing. She was free and clear, it seemed. She floated up, clearing hundreds of stories worth of code in seconds. At the top of the stacks, a beacon of encrypted text over each identified the specific node. She put the best decryption bot her poor little PCom could handle to work. She was looking for flight control VI for an off-books shuttle from an off-books facility.

Starfire should have felt them coming before she saw them. With her rig at home, the hi-fi network connection she managed to pay for every month, she would have. It's one of the things that put her in a category above most of her contemporaries, her gut. She felt the prickling at the back of her neck, even when such a thing had not been programmed into the neural network. Nobody knew quite how it worked, but the top tier of hackers could do it nonetheless.

Active black ICE, and a lot of it. Black ICE: intrusion countermeasure electronics that could create a feedback loop in her neural connection that literally electrocuted her brain through the cables with which she'd jacked in. Another piece of terminology that had taken its name from twentieth century science fiction, a fact which made the reality of her situation no less stark.

She had never seen active black ICE before. Passive black ICE, yes of course. Firewalls to keep out roving bands of hackers with the threat of death. Crackable, but only with a *lot* of know-how and months to prepare. These walls were built around every major corporate network in cyberspace. But active black ICE? The kind that hunted black hats like Selina? Her contemporaries hoped never to have these kinds of encounters.

The head of WalCo OpSec must have a poetic streak, she thought, because unlike the stacks, the active black ICE *had* been skinned. To the visual input of her neural connection, Selina saw over a dozen massive ravens, flapping lazily through the stacks, from the center towards the peripheral. They hadn't spotted her yet, thanks to her cloaking program, but it was only a matter of seconds.

No users in the stacks, and this much bandwidth devoted to active black ICE? Starfire held no lingering doubt that the backdoor had been a trap. They'd probably left it open, but with a tripwire of sorts. Odds were good that if she returned, she would find only more passive black ICE blocking her way. *Stupid.* If she'd had more time, she could have spotted it, gotten around it. But there wasn't more time. Slowing down would be tantamount to failure. And anyway, no point in dwelling on things she could have done. There were only seconds left in the here-and-now.

Black ICE bearing down on her, what to do? She could pull a hard eject – message Gash in the real world to physically pull the plug. There were a lot of downsides to this plan. For one thing, severing the connection to a neural network without properly logging out had inherent biological dangers. It disoriented the user for hours in a best-case scenario and had been known to cause serious brain damage. The neurons were not made for experiencing a virtual world as a physical world, but they were *especially* not made for going from one to the other without buffering.

Even worse than that, a hard eject would leave an after-image of her that a first day network security specialist could trace within minutes. By itself, that wasn't the worst thing in the world, since they were already on the way to Rhodes; but, given that her plan had been to fabricate new target data for the WalCo team, to send them to the Balkans or Turkey, it would be a guaranteed mission failure.

Mission failure wasn't an option for Starfire, because mission failure meant death to her team. And yet, according to the parameters of her op, she'd hit mission failure the moment they detected her intrusion. *Fine,* she thought. If the mission had failed, it was time to change the mission. An idea took shape, and the notion of it, the sheer brutality of it turned her stomach. But it was them or her, and it wasn't going to be her.

No time to think, the black ICE was on her and she had a new plan. First, she needed to buy herself a few more seconds. Starfire had four decoy bots on standby, each a slight variation on the same theme. To the untrained eye, the code spoke to an obvious purpose – burrow at random into decrypted files and steal data. Secondary programming provided for the bots to replicate rapidly. The "primary" purpose of these bots, in truth, were to be decoys. Not in fifty years could one of these bots, unchecked, crack into a security network like WalCo's. But that wasn't the point.

Starfire unleashed them all at once, and as one the flock of black ICE programs turned. In a single heartbeat, the nearest ICE had almost reached her decoys, missiles streaking towards chaff. One such program could quickly destroy a dozen such bots. But in that same heartbeat, each bot had multiplied three dozen times over. Within a few seconds, there were hundreds of decoy bots bouncing idiotically around the stacks, the black ICE ravens gobbling them up even as they spawned more copies.

It would not last, but she had bought herself a moment. She checked in on her decryption program. She had a partial list of directories, but no time to sift through it to find the specific stack that held data for air control. What she did have was one more trick up her sleeve: a bloodhound program she'd written once, a pattern sniffer. And she had a particular set of forty digits, changing in precisely the same way each second, as the troop transport travelled at a fixed velocity across the Atlantic. WalCo would have all the data encrypted, and at least a dozen aircraft out at once. But, assuming WalCo only had one troop transport deployed, flying at top speeds, then the bloodhound would find an encrypted series of forty digits changing at just the right speed. And then she would have them.

Selina keyed the appropriate pattern into the bloodhound program as quickly as she could on her PCom. All of the data passing through it, or maybe the low bandwidth of the satellite wifi in the boonies, *something* was slowing her down. It was not like at home, the technology was lagging behind her thought process. And the black ICE was devouring her decoys faster than they could replicate. It would only be a matter of seconds before they were on her, and she was jerking in her meat back in the real world, electricity turning her brain to char. The end, game over compadre. She gritted her teeth and worked. This would work or it wouldn't. Just work.

She had it. The digital "scent" programmed in, the bloodhound streaked off into the stacks, a small blue light beneath colossal towers of green data. The black ICE ignored it. A human operator might have been able to distinguish between a hundred distractions and one program with purpose. But to the automated ICE programs, it all looked the same. And that was why Selina was going to win – the big corporations all relied too much on automation, didn't understand the value of an intuitive human, of guts, of instincts, of the animal brain that takes over in the moments before death and does more than a machine could ever dream of to live. To win. Selina followed her bloodhound, the stacks of numbers emerald rain drops flowing around her at the speed of light, more ravens moving in her periphery, descending on her decoys with ravenous efficiency, the flurry of destruction all around her now.

But then she was there. She slid into the center of one of the stacks, like all the others, and there was the data. Encrypted, so she had no way of being sure that it was the same continually changing string of forty numbers. But the frequency matched, so what else could it be?

There was no time for delicate work here. No chance to trick the transport or send them somewhere else, because when she was done, she would *have* to eject. Starfire fought back the urge to second-guess. She readied a program every black hat carried, but one she'd never had cause to use. And then she nuked the whole stack. A program designed not to break security or extract data, but to enter a datastream and wantonly change it. Like a fast-acting cancer, it would mutate the data until it had been completely ruined. Data would be irretrievable – to anyone – and computer programs with primary lines of code nuked would be unable to function.

Starfire watched the grainy satellite display of the troop transport. If she had succeeded, then the men and women on that shuttle would have only seconds to register their deaths, the flight computer cutting out without warning. Navigation, propulsion, gone. Sure enough, the black dot dropped out of the sky, hitting the water at thousands of km/h. A bright flash as the forces at work ripped the shuttle apart and the engine exploded. And then the feed cut entirely. Hemmingway must have been watching, after all.

Dead. Those people were dead. Selina had just become a mass murderer. But even as her heart wrenched itself sideways, she knew there was no time to dwell on it. The last few decoys were being gobbled up by WalCo's lethal ravens, the programs turning beady eyes towards Starfire. She'd finally been detected.

Pull the plug. She sent the message to Gash's PCom. He only had maybe five seconds to receive and comply.

If she was lucky. With nothing left in the world to devour but her, the flock of dark ravens streaked towards her – impossibly fast. She had nothing left but to run. She turned and raced away from the ICE, deeper into the stacks. They were faster, but maybe she could juke them. She turned left, then right, then she was practically face to face with one of the Black ICE programs, its digital talons reaching towards her. She dropped, plummeting to the digital pavement below. The programs were all around her now, descending from all angles. Nowhere left to go, nowhere left to run. She was going to fry. She was going to –

Everything collapsed and then expanded. The whole universe shone brilliant white, blinding and burning her eyes. A horrendous screeching, like nails on a chalkboard inside of her head, magnified a thousand times. Gash's face in front of her, the black ICE ravens roaring towards her like feathered bullets, the two worlds interposed over each other, an infinity mirror in her brain.

And then, nothing.

GASH

She was alive. Unconscious, but alive. That's what Gash tried to focus on. Blood trickled periodically from her nose, and he wiped it away with a shred of torn cloth from one of the White Lotus robes.

Gash had no medical experience, but his PCom featured the standard medical diagnostic tool. He followed the first time user's guide, inputting her symptoms and using the PCom's standard and thermal imager to scan her. Body temp, heart rate, radiation levels, hydration levels, all on the digital display. The app's virtual intelligence walked him through a few basic tests. When it was all done, the device declared her healthy. She would wake soon.

Not that it mattered. He felt pulled in half a dozen directions. There was an overriding concern for her health. But beyond that, he longed to pick up where they'd left off, while at the same time recognizing how magnificently bad an idea that would be. Hooking up with a young woman half his age, who also happened to be his charge as bodyguard? She had more than enough shit going on in her life without him making it all worse. Not to mention they'd not yet known each other for one whole month. But that had always been

Nagash Jensen's way. He fell for women that he shouldn't, and he never forgot or moved on, only added to the growing list. Lulu and Serena, for instance. A couple dozen from before the Serena days (and some during) that he still remembered. And now Selina. Most of these went unmentioned and unreciprocated, simple memories of everyday encounters and the accompanying quiet yearning. But this one he'd solidified. He'd kissed her.

He shook his head and stood. *Focus on the mission,* he thought. Get Selina back home safe, get papers from Hemmingway. There would be a woman waiting for him when he finally settled down in one of the boomtowns in Scotland, Norway, or on the coast of Greenland. Maybe one of the arcologies in Antarctica built around one of the dozen spaceports in the Kessler window. Normal winters, mild summers, a happy life. Just had to get there without messing anything up.

SAGE

Sage could not get a feel for this Frederick person that now guided them and Hiro through the city of Rhodes. He'd been nothing but helpful, if anxious to get back to his people, but something that Sage could not put their finger on didn't quite seem right.

No matter, they had bigger concerns than that at this point. It became clear that Frederick was guiding them towards the great big castle in the middle of the city. An old-looking Gothic construction that seemed out of place amid the stubs of twentieth century Mediterranean homes, which were themselves out of place in this era, in which space could always be sold at a premium and modernization dictated all.

"How many Hospitallers are in this castle?" Sage asked.

Frederick stopped walking long enough to look at them and shrug. "No idea. Listen, we've only been here like a day. I can tell you that they have enough manpower that they *run* this city. Every other possible authority is long-gone from this place, but the Hospitallers have complete control. No terrorists, no corporate interests."

"What about this 'White Lotus'?" Hiro asked.

A look passed between Frederick and Hiro before Frederick answered. "They seem to be in charge of the countryside, but not the city." What had that been? Sage saw nothing on Hiro's face, perhaps it had only been in their head.

The group came to a stop half a block from the front of the castle. In the hazy red light of the just-rising sun, it looked exactly like a castle ought to. Twin stone towers like two white Chess rooks flanked the great stone doors in the center. Red-clad figures stood atop the parapets with assault rifles, not paying specific attention to the people on the ground below, but generally on high alert for anything out of the ordinary.

"I don't think we should just go knock on the door," Hiro said.

"Are you sure?" Frederick laughed.

Sage didn't know what to do. These people had tons of manpower, and clearly they were up to no good. But they and Hiro were rogue, acting against orders from the higher-ups in Interpol. Could they get backup? How many of these self-styled Knights were actually criminals, and what sort of statutes could they be charged under? It made Sage's head throb.

"Um, listen," Frederick said, interrupting Sage's thoughts. "I need to get going. It's vital that I be there when Selina and Gash go into the Pit. I just wanted to show you the Hospitaller HQ. Not much else I can do for you, except warn you that most people on the island are with these guys, whether they want to be or not."

"Thanks," Sage said. "We're grateful for your assistance."

Frederick was gone before Sage finished the sentence. So strange.

Sage felt a hand, tentative on their shoulder.

"They're starting to take notice of us, partner," Hiro said.

It was true. The men on the towers looked down at them directly now, and spoke into their wrists, reporting suspicious activity to others of their order.

"We better back off and regroup," Sage said.

Back through the streets they travelled, quickly but not too quickly. Eventually, Sage led them into a small café with a sign in Greek that they couldn't read, but with a picture of a coffee cup – a universal symbol that transcended language.

A few people, even at this hour, sat on tiny wrought-iron chairs at small round tables, sipping coffee and reading or speaking in low voices. Sage and Hiro ordered coffees themselves and sat. Before they could take the first sip, though, the door opened and Hospitallers came through. Eight of them total, they filed in quietly. Without saying anything, the other patrons calmly rose and left once the way was clear. The men did not acknowledge these people at all. They fiddled benignly with rifles and handguns until the shop had been cleared of customers. Even the proprietor stepped into the back room and closed the door.

Ten people remained. Sage, Hiro, and the Knights Hospitaller, formerly the Knights of Rhodes, all men in long red jackets with gunpowder weapons of an earlier age. Nobody spoke, but they knew that these men were here to kill them, and that the odds were stacked badly against the two freelancing Interpol agents.

Sage slowly reached under the table and unholstered their weapons. *Everyone dies sometime*, they thought.

SELINA

Waking came slowly to Selina. A headache pounded through the corridors of her brain, and she could smell crusted blood in her nasal passageways. She sat up, shielding tender eyes from the harsh white of the little LED lantern, and there was Gash, looking at her with puppy dog eyes. All of their stuff was packed and stacked, ready to go.

"How long have I been out?" she asked.

"Just a few hours. How do you feel?"

"Like my brain is trying to claw free of my skull."

He laughed a single laugh, long and harsh. Then grew serious. "You're lucky you didn't do any serious damage. I'm lucky I don't have to live with something like that." He opened his mouth as if to say more, but then turned away.

"Any more word on WalCo?"

"Hemmingway hasn't called, if that's what you mean. I'm sure they'll send more, though."

Selina thought about this. He was right. WalCo had near-infinite resources, and was known to be relentless. Next time, the weaknesses she had exposed in their network would be gone. Next time they would be dead. "Well then we'd better work fast," she said.

"I've got everything packed up, but I think you should rest."

"There's no time. Grab me some pain pills from my bag for this headache. We've got to meet Frederick for our initial survey of the Pit. If we can, we'll have to round up a crew with some heavy duty equipment to actually get in there. But I want to get eyes on the site first."

"It may not be today or tomorrow, but WalCo will be back. Do you still think there's time for an expedition?"

"We've come a long way and killed a *lot* of people to get here." Selina looked down at the floor. Saying the words aloud, it really hit home. Her stun gun had been set permanently to lethal since arriving on this island. Why even bother with a stun gun? Selina Kan had always been many things: Thief, black hat (same thing, really), scrapper. She'd put her fair share of people into hospitals and street clinics in her day but had never been a taker of lives. Now she had a body count to rival most serial killers.

Gash handed her a couple of pain pills, and she popped these, choking them back dry.

"I'm not giving up until I absolutely have to. We'll keep finding a way, somehow."

"You're the boss, boss."

With that, they hefted their gear and made their way back out into the world. But, Selina vowed, she would be back for that relic, the lost foot of the Colossus of Rhodes.

SELINA

Gash and Selina had opted to travel on foot. Gas automobiles were ostentatious, and they didn't have a clue what they'd be stumbling into when they actually got to the coordinates of the Pit.

It did not take long for Selina to regret that choice. The afternoon sun pounded them ruthlessly, and though it lacked the lung-filling humidity of the Florida summer, it felt as though the sun flayed micro-layers from her skin with each step she took. They did not speak as they walked the blasted Mediterranean landscape, and nothing moved around them but the shimmering lines of heat rising between them and the horizon.

Selina tracked their progress as a small blue dot on a GPS map using the ambient Wi-Fi. They drew nearer.

She crested a rise, Gash just behind her, to a surprise. As expected, the land above the Pit was indistinguishable from the rest of the land. Unexpectedly, someone had already set up here. Large canvas tents dotted the landscape, clustered particularly on the eastern border of the Pit below. One particularly massive tent hummed, a low baritone rumble that Selina could hear even from this considerable distance, and she guessed that there might be some kind of laser drill within. Such a piece of equipment *had* supposedly been stolen from the city long before the arrival of her team. Were the White Lotus already drilling at her site? No way *that* was a coincidence.

There didn't seem to be anybody present, so she started down the ridge towards the camp. Where had they gone? Where, for that matter, was Frederick? She hoped he had not been caught, waiting for her to wake up. Behind, Gash huffed and mumbled, out of breath. Probably hurting from his injury. She ignored it, merely gesturing for him to follow.

They were about halfway down when something whistled just over her head. When she turned to follow the trajectory, she saw an arrow buried in the dry earth. And then it detonated, knocking her to her feet and showering her with dirt and rocks. Another arrow found a home in the ground just beside her head. She rolled just far enough out of the way that when it exploded, the worst she got was ringing ears. Gash had already found his feet and pulled her to hers when the third arrow went wide. But now she could clearly see a number of forms in white robes materializing out of the tall brush on either side of the White Lotus camp. And then, a flash of red in her peripheral vision, and a loud crack; the unmistakable battle cry of gunpowder.

Gash tackled her back to the dry earth, landing on top of her, shielding her with his body. She tried to squirm free, but he was much larger than she was.

They were caught directly in a crossfire, as gunfire erupted, and the whistle of arrows multiplied over their heads. Hospitallers were launching an assault on the White Lotus camp at exactly this moment. Had their meddling accelerated the conflict? The White Lotus had turned their attention to the Hospitaller army pouring over the hill on the west side of the Pit. At least two dozen of the red-cloaked men and women streamed like trickling blood across the blasted Mediterranean landscape, finding cover in the brush. Exploding arrows took a few Knights out, but they pushed forward, firing in unison at the White Lotus, some of the white-robed figures dropping as well.

Gash's plan, evidently, amounted to little more than giving up his own life for hers, using his body as a shield. But what then? Someone would win this battle, and whoever won, they were an enemy to Gash and Selina. They had to escape but standing would make them a target. It would be useless to try to formulate a plan with her bodyguard in the sudden cacophony of a battle closing in around them, but they *had* to do *something.*

Then there came a sound, distinct from the battle. A deafening boom from far above the field rattled Selina's bones and shook the Earth. Gash looked up long enough for her to squirm out from under. The entire battle had frozen, Hospitallers and White Lotus alike stared up into the sky. And then it was upon them. With all the force of a missile, a great metal cylinder struck the ground directly between the two battle lines. The whole world shuddered with the impact, and a geyser of dirt and debris blasted up and into the air from the force of it. The thing stood almost ten feet tall, rising out of its own crater. Steam poured off it in sheets as it cooled from its rapid descent. The thing was a simple gun-metal grey, except that spray-painted across the side in red were the following letters: "V-A-L-K-Y-R-I-E." Servos whined, a panel slid away from the front, and a humanoid figure almost eight feet tall emerged from within, striding out of the crater in two great steps.

"Valkyrie," Gash breathed, a child speaking the name of his favorite comic book hero. A young boy speaking the name of the boogeyman. Valkyrie. Selina did not speak but felt the same awe in the breath she held within her lungs. Even without the clearly written moniker on the low-orbit deployment pod, this could be none other than *the* Valkyrie, a world-famous merc piloting a prototype exo-suit that had been spotted on only the highest-stakes, highest-profile corporate battlefields. The wars for the last oil fields, the Canadian War of Independence, at diamond mines in Angola during the turmoil there a year ago.

She was magnificent. A mechanized humanoid, piloted by *someone* inside (nobody knew the true identity of Valkyrie). Sleek metal arms and legs, painted crimson, led up to a metal visage of a Norse warrior woman – a gunmetal face stylized in a grimace, and with two great wings rising from the "helmet" atop her head. The eyes glowed blue from within. She spun a massive spear and rammed it into the ground. Her signature entrance, rounded out by several heavy metal chords that blared from speakers set into the side of the suit's head. A warning to all that might oppose her to run. They would not receive mercy if they chose to stand and fight.

What was she doing *here* of all places? Had the Hospitallers or the White Lotus hired her? Could they afford her? If so, Selina was in deeper than she had imagined. And that was pretty damn deep.

At first, Selina thought the White Lotus were the ones who'd hired the merc. Valkyrie turned towards the Knights, who'd already begun to fire on her. She pointed her spear, and dozens of micro-charges blossomed from the sides, roaring towards the Hospitaller battle lines, detonating in a chain of explosions that tossed red-jacketed bodies like little rag-dolls. The survivors scattered, returning fire.

But then an arrow struck the exo-suit directly from behind, exploding with the impact. Valkyrie shuddered but did not slow. She spun to face these new attackers and a small minigun rose like a wrist ornament from within the arm of the suit, already spinning up. A few more arrows landed at her feet, but she strode through the explosions, the minigun screaming now, the blue tracer fire of a thousand gauss flechettes per minute streaming like water towards the White Lotus attackers, chewing through them with the ferocity of a school of piranhas. They never stood a chance.

Who the hell was she here for? The amount of money needed to deploy *her* boggled the mind. Yesterday, Selina could not have dreamed of a shuttle full of WalCo black ops descending on Rhodes. Today, though, she had *killed* a shuttle full of WalCo black ops and perhaps the only operative with more firepower than even that stood before her, fighting all of her enemies. Gash broke her reverie, pulling her to her feet and back towards the ridge.

"Whatever this is," he said, "it's our cue to get to safety."

She pulled free of his grasp. "No. It's our chance to get into that tent and see how much digging the White Lotus have already done."

"Are you crazy?" Gash shouted over the sounds of battle, and the cries of the wounded and dying. "That's fucking *Valkyrie.* If she so much as looks at us, we're dead. This mission of yours has just risen from 'bad idea' status to 'suicide mission.' I'm not taking *her* on with a damn *revolver.*"

While Gash spoke, Valkyrie had been finishing up the White Lotus. The remaining Hospitallers had closed the distance, still firing at her. The bullets that struck her armor glanced off, doing precisely nothing. It would take some serious artillery to get through *that* armor. But Selina had to give them credit for courage, they weren't giving up.

Valkyrie turned back to the last aggressors, and two flaps opened at her back. A brief explosion of jet propellant sent her sailing up into the air, and then back down into the midst of the Hospitallers. Here, in close quarters, her spear truly functioned as a spear, as she impaled the nearest of the Knights. Even point blank, their weapons on full auto, bullets ricocheted harmlessly from exo-suit. Some of the bravest of them leapt at her, drawing melee weapons of their own.

If Selina had learned one thing about the Hospitallers, it was that they all favored body enhancements. But even with increased strength and swords of their own, they could do nothing to Valkyrie. She whirled about, skewering and disemboweling men with frightening efficiency, as sword strokes glanced off the impenetrable sheet of metal that protected the flesh of the pilot within.

"Now," Selina called to Gash, "is our chance." And she sprinted for the large, humming tent. Gash called out, but she knew he would follow. And if he didn't, well, too bad. She drew her stun gun, set permanently these last days to "lethal," in case she ran into any stragglers in the camp. Or in case Valkyrie found them out. Not that her little stun darts would have a remote chance of effecting that exo-suit.

Selina leapt over several dead White Lotus, trying not to look too closely at the mess of gore, trying not to slip on any of it in her haste. She was almost there, twenty meters from the tent, when she heard another explosion, and looked up just in time to see Valkyrie landing in front of her.

Up close, she was even more imposing. A head and half taller than Selina, fully covered in alloyed metals, those glowing blue eyes malevolent by design. Gash, who had followed Selina's mad dash after all, pointed his revolver at her head; she swatted it away with the back half of her spear. He pulled his knife from his boot and lunged for her, but she grabbed him by the wrist and simply held him suspended in the air, while he chopped meaninglessly at her armored arm.

"Be still," Valkyrie said, the voice booming from the speakers around her head metallic and lacking inflection in the truest sense. "I'm not here to kill you. I was hired to help you."

Gash stopped at that, and she let him down.

So much coursed through Selina's head. The improbable providence of her life. Her father, a working stiff, stumbling onto the long lost journal of a French explorer. Her journey through adolescence, the fascination with Rhodes that had arisen out of that simple book. The discovery of the Pit, the acceptance of her grant to go out and study it. Hemmingway pairing her with an almost super-soldier and the ridiculous frequency with which they had survived encounters they shouldn't have. And now this, the most expensive, most-sought-out mercenary on the global market lands in the middle of a war just above the Pit, which Selina had been building towards studying for decades of her life. And has been hired to help *her*. She didn't have this kind of money. Not even Hemmingway, with his occasionally altruistic impulses towards her, could have arranged something like this.

This was corporate money. Big time. No other explanation.

—

"Who hired you to help me? Why? Why now, when we've had half a dozen brushes with death already?"

Valkyrie held her armored hand up and shook her metal head. "I'm paid per-engagement. You haven't needed me until now and won't need me again. You'll clean up those stragglers inside that tent, and you'll make your discovery. I can't answer any of your other questions, but based on the file I read, you're not likely to give up just because you know someone else has had a hand in getting you here." Was that a tone of admiration? From the greatest warrior of Selina's generation?

Before Gash could say a word or Selina could respond again, Valkyrie reached up and grasped a cable travelling through the air at extreme speed. Selina saw that it was attached to a large transport shuttle roaring overhead at full speed. When Valkyrie's metal fingers clamped around the cable, some kind of internal magnets locked her in place, and she was lifted with a jolt into the air. She receded to a dot within seconds, and before a minute had elapsed, the tiny form of her had disappeared into the clouds with the plane that had picked her up.

Later, Selina suspected, a crew would be on hand to retrieve her orbital descent pod. This would be repaired and shuttled with her back up to her satellite base, where it would be prepared for the next engagement, to which she could be dispatched within moments, no matter the location.

All around, in her wake, was carnage. Dead Hospitallers and White Lotus littered the field, blood everywhere. Only Selina and Gash remained standing, except there was Frederick appearing from hiding on the far ridge with gun in hand.

When she turned back to the tent, Gash had picked up his revolver and was closing the distance to it in long strides. She wanted to call out to him, to stop him, but she knew somehow that it was just fine.

GASH

Nagash Jensen had never felt a bloodlust quite so profound before, as he cleared the distance to the main tent in the White Lotus camp in full sprint. He hoped there would be White Lotus remaining in the tent, his body ached with the desire to spill blood. Was it the impotence of his encounter with Valkyrie? Was it because he had been usurped in his role as the protector and savior? Was it the previous brush with death, or the fact that Selina had almost been killed as well? Was it something else entirely? Possibilities rolled through his head, many and varied, each arriving in force and each as fleeting as the spring squalls back home in Washington, from before the weather went fully to shit.

It didn't matter. There was nothing but the tent ahead, the throbbing in his side, the revolver in his right hand and the knife in his left. When he pushed inside, he counted five White Lotus. In the center of the space stood something that looked like a giant telescope, only inverted. It stood above and pointed down at a hole in the ground like a great three-legged spider. It hummed loudly, and a blinding beam of white energy streamed out of it and into the hole.

They were digging. Apparently, Selina wasn't the first to have that idea about the Pit. All five White Lotus dropped everything and circled him with swords in hand.

He dropped the first two with blasts to the chest, before the other three were on him, arcing swords flashing in the bright light of the industrial laser. He rolled away, his heart singing, the wound in his side all but forgotten and the pain of it something for a distant version of himself. In the moment there was nothing but blood. Blood pulsing within his own veins, blood pouring out of the White Lotus as he carved them up one by one with his knife. A blood-red filter between his eyes and the world, painting everything bloody as he felled the last White Lotus. More. Where were the rest? MORE. But there were no rest. It was all he could do to restrain himself, holster his weapons, when Selina and Frederick joined him in the tent. He could almost *smell* their blood in their arteries. Frederick's eyes were wide still, but Selina had just watched Valkyrie do her work, and barely gave a second glance to the carnage within.

Gash's chest heaved, and he closed his eyes. Deep breaths. Calm. He had never let this side of him out for so much time at once, and it wanted to take full control, banish the other version of himself to the corners of his mind forever. It yearned for blood. No, thirsted. It thirsted for blood and shook the walls of his mind with that desire. Blood covered him, blood dripped from the furniture in half a dozen places, he need only bend down or lean in and have a little sip. His body pulled him towards the nearest pool of the deep crimson stuff. He opened his mind to the pain in his side, the wound from before. The pain flooded back in and he welcomed it, using it to clear away the frenzy that had descended on him.

SAGE

Sage looked each of the Hospitallers over in turn. In the moment before they attacked, everything had frozen in motion. Each of the burly knights sported some form of facial hair, from the five o'clock shadow to a full survival beard. Each brandished a different form of weaponry from the previous century. A few also bore scabbards with sheathed blades on belts that could be seen in fleeting glances beneath their flapping red overcoats. The men were all white, of varied European ancestry. They put them mostly as Italians and Frenchmen, but probably each of the flags of Western Europe found representation within their soon-to-be attackers.

"Boys," Sage said. "Can we talk about this?" Their fingers hovered inches from the grips of their weapons, ready to draw the moment one of them moved.

Hiro only cracked his knuckles and smiled.

"You've been after our leader, Gerard, for years." One of the men, burlier than the rest, spoke up. "And you're here spying on us with a White Lotus? I think talking is out of the question."

Sage looked over at Hiro. A White Lotus? There was the glimmer in his eyes, that same glimmer as always. He gave a soft chuckle. "Do all Asians look the same to you Knights?"

They all drew at once. The Hospitallers lifted their weapons to fire. Sage kicked over the table and dove, both weapons in hand and firing as they did.

A spray of bullets ricocheted off the iron tables, chewing up the plaster on the far wall and digging up the tile all around Sage. Their gauss flechettes made short work of two of the Hospitallers.

For his part, Hiro moved like a ghost. Sage had never seen him actually fighting until that moment. He never drew a weapon, but in the time it took Sage to take cover and blow away two Hospitallers, he had danced his way across the coffee shop and spun around one of the armed gunmen, breaking his neck and using him as a body shield to absorb the bullets of several others.

By the time Sage rolled to their feet and plugged another of the Hospitallers, Hiro had worked his way through the remaining four, his hands moving too fast for the eye to follow, each time striking once and each time a bio-enhanced shooter dropping to the ground, stone-dead.

The smoke of gunfire and the dust of old plaster hung in the air, a white cloud that reeked of sulfur and chalk. Blood trickled down Sage's left cheek, and they reached up to feel the source. Just a shallow wound above their ear, they had been grazed by a piece of shrapnel or a bullet had come a few inches from striking home in their brain.

In about ten seconds, they'd killed eight armed and enhanced criminals. Sage took a deep breath and looked at Hiro. He dusted off his hands and re-adjusted his tie.

"You sure you're not White Lotus, partner? You moved faster than I've ever seen a human being move." Sage was half joking, but half not. They knew Hiro was special from the way he'd handled himself before. But they had never actually seen him in motion before, and it truly had seemed to be something super-human.

Hiro placed a hand on Sage's elbow, gently, almost like

someone's grandfather taking them gently aside.

"Sage," he said. "I was assigned to you; your fourth partner, I might add. We're both Interpol, or were until *you* decided we had to chase this secret organization rather than return to the Home Office and take our new assignment. You know I'm not a member of a secret society of ninjas. I told you, I just so happen to remember countless former lives, and it's been my fortune – or misfortune, I might argue on certain days – to have been a warrior for many lifetimes."

"I know," Sage said. "But you took them apart *hard*. You sure you're not enhanced?"

Hiro's smile could only be described as serene. "I am enhanced in a way that technology could never achieve."

"What does that mean, exactly? Because of your so-called past lives, you have more experience?"

"Listen, I have the feeling that their HQ is largely emptied out just now."

Sage only looked quizzically at Hiro.

"Call it a hunch," he said.

"We should be dead right now. I'm not so sure that going back to the enemy's stronghold is the best idea."

"Okay," Hiro said, sitting gingerly in one of the coffee shop's wrought-iron chairs. "What would you like to do instead? Shall we return to Paris and let this all play out without us?"

Sage's face flushed. They could not tell exactly the source. Shame at their fear? Anger at the prospect of leaving this unfinished? What even was "this" anyway? They had chased Gerard for so long, only to discover now that there was a whole castle full of Gerards waging war against another secret society, and for what?

Sage considered their other options. Call Interpol HQ and have them come get them and Hiro? Would they send reinforcements, or would they simply arrest Sage and Hiro without asking any questions? How long would it take to get reinforcements, and what would the Hospitallers be doing in the mean time? These people had kept their presence from the world for centuries.

"Okay," Sage said. "Since you've got all those past lives roiling around beneath the surface, I'll trust that hunch of yours. Let's head back to the castle and see if we can... well shit, I don't even know what we're going to try to do."

Hiro lifted his shoulders in another shrug, the Buddha on his tie doing a little dance to the motion. "Let's try to find the leader of the Hospitallers and get some answers. Maybe we can bring him in and use him to get Interpol bought into the idea of finding the rest of them."

Sage nodded. "You've got a level head, Hiro. I admire that. Let's go find Gerard's successor and bring him in."

VALKYRIE

"You're sure the public caught wind of your operation in Rhodes?"

Valkyrie laughed, long and hard. She laughed so hard that tears formed in the corners of her eyes. She looked at the man, fully aware that he could not reciprocate. He wore a suit and tie. Generic. Grey hair showed him to be of advanced age, but he'd positioned himself with a backlight so that his face remained shaded, and she could not identify his features. Still, he would be seeing even less – a conference or de-brief with Valkyrie did *not* come with visuals. She spoke softly into the microphone built into her exo-suit, but all the man would see on his screen for visual would be black. Nobody saw her face but her doctors and technicians.

"Listen, I monitor my media presence very closely. My reputation is my greatest asset. But I don't think you understand. There are media satellites tasked solely with the job of observing my orbital station. When my ODP deployed, half a dozen techs in every news-media conglomerate immediately began triangulating my trajectory, and swarms of writers commenced co-creating op-eds speculating where I was going and why. Within an hour, stories of

Valkyrie in Rhodes will have been shared and re-shared in ten million iterations across the blogosphere."

"I see," he said.

"Listen up Mr. 'Smith,' you hired *the* most famous mercenary on the planet to do this job. You could have had a team of ex black-ops on the site, but you chose to have a mystery-woman in a robot suit launched from space instead. Why?"

He stiffened.

"Of course, you don't have to tell me, but don't be so shocked at my lack of professionalism. I can decimate an army of forty heavily-armed hostiles in three minutes, that's my main selling point. Curiosity is a vice, and people who are satisfied with my work often feel validated in indulging it."

He chuckled. "I admire your audacity. I wish we could meet in person. This cloak and dagger business is so unappealing."

"You know –" she started.

"I know you don't meet with anyone. Greater men than I have tried." He paused. "I'm happy to indulge your curiosity, at least as far as I can. Why you? I suppose the same reason that anyone hires you for your particularly flamboyant brand of decimation. To make a statement to the world."

Valkyrie watched. The silhouette of the man never moved, but she sensed a keen sort of emotional energy coming off of him. "What kind of statement?" she asked.

"Selina, whom you helped to survive, is about to unearth a very old secret. Something terrible, done to the world centuries ago. Your service has not only paved the way to that, but also helped to ensure that the watchful eyes of the world will never leave Rhodes, and that this travesty will not be repeated."

"It's clear she doesn't work for you. Or at least doesn't know that she does. What makes you so sure she'll do what you hope she's going to?" Valkyrie asked.

Though she couldn't see his face, she felt sure that 'Mr. Smith' was smiling. "Because we've made arrangements with one of her

—

travelling companions."

Below her, the world shrank away. The island of Rhodes receded from the horizon. The Mediterranean stretched out beneath her, the crystal blue of it serene from this height. She was struck by the notion, as always, that from here the world did not seem to be concerned with the trials and tribulations of humanity, the bloodshed and the savagery, the machinations and plans. From here she was reminded that the world abided humanity, frail things flickering across its surface for a brief moment and disappearing in a flash. No matter that she was keenly aware of the triteness of the thought, each time she had it. From up here it did not matter how many had thought it before or would think it again. From up here, she felt oh-so very small in the universe.

SELINA

Selina tapped for a few minutes at the display for the laser drill. When she pulled the status update, blood rushed to her face, and she clapped once. The White Lotus had been drilling for a long time, and they were just about through. The laser had penetrated 1,004 meters into the ground. It was angled slightly, to break through just on the edge of the pit, and there was less than a full meter of rock to go before it was through.

A mining laser such as this lost digging efficiency as the mining depth grew larger, but it would nevertheless be only a matter of minutes before the sensors on the apparatus dinged that the desired depth – programmed by the White Lotus or perhaps by some kidnapped Rhodian labor – had been achieved. She turned to face Gash and Frederick.

"Listen, you two. They've been drilling for a long time, and they're almost through. I just want to take a second to let you both know that I appreciate everything you've done to get us here so far. I know I promised you something vastly different from this when you signed up. I can't even begin to comprehend the full scope of what we've entered into. Secret organizations trying to kill us, a celebrity mercenary inexplicably showing up to help us, and now a giant pit leading deep into the Earth."

"Don't forget the hidden temple secretly housing a piece of the ancient Colossus of Rhodes!" Frederick chimed in, suddenly too happy.

"That too," Selina agreed.

Gash shrugged. "It's okay, seems like life and death situations follow me wherever I go."

Astounding, how that man could go from berserker to quiet acceptance in an instant.

"Now I'm going to ask even more of you. In a moment, this drill breaks through into an ancient pit, deep in the ground. I'm not sure how it ties into the collapse of the Colossus, or the Knights of Rhodes. I'm not sure why the White Lotus are digging here, or how it ties into their apparent belief that magic was stolen from the world. But I mean to find out. The gear on hand will allow us to descend with ropes and climbing harnesses all the way down to the Pit's entrance, but I don't know what we'll do from there. We may have to climb down without safety gear, because the ropes the White Lotus have on hand will only get us to the Pit's entrance. And it goes *much* deeper than that. How deep, I don't know.

"You've both risked so much for me already. I don't want you to follow me on what could well be a suicide mission for any reasons but your own." She looked at Frederick. "You just signed on to be my assistant for an expedition linking a benign natural phenomenon to some old folk legends. You've been shot at and by now probably figured out that absolutely nothing I told you when I hired you was fully true. Do you want to leave?"

Frederick looked taken aback. "Are you kidding me? Whatever we find down there is going to change the entire world. How could I possibly miss out on that?"

His face burned with passion bordering on zealotry. He'd always been a bit of an enigma, but now more than ever Selina felt like she had no idea who this young man was. Nevertheless, he'd made his wishes clear. He was coming. She turned to Gash. Her voice caught when she tried to ask him the same question.

He reached out to her with a hand but froze and, after a moment, thought better of it. "I signed on as your bodyguard. I've gotten a bit more than I bargained for, true, but I wouldn't be much of a bodyguard if I let you descend alone into a mysterious pit into the center of the Earth without me."

"Well," Selina said. "It won't go all the way into the center of the Earth. We'd be incinerated in the Mantle long before we ever got near the center of the Earth. But we might be descending deeper into the crust than any other person has gone before."

He rolled his eyes and made to say something, but before he could, the mining drill gave off a happy sort of chime, before powering off.

It was done. A deep pit, undiscovered for centuries because of its relatively small size and great depth, leading down and down, unsealed for the first time in modern history. Or ever.

She practically sprinted to the drill's control panel and entered a handful of commands. It retracted fully, and stepped itself away from the hole, clearing the path for her little expedition to enter.

The White Lotus had already arranged five spools of carbon nanotube cable, thin and nearly indestructible, long enough to lower them the full kilometer into the pit. What had the White Lotus expected to do from there? Selina didn't know and didn't have time to consider. She just had to get down there, the need for answers consumed her now, and her cautious impulses were swept aside in a torrent of exhilaration.

She deployed three of the spools, tossing climbing harnesses to Frederick and Gash, before clamping herself into a harness of her own. Frederick was able to get into his own harness with ease, but Gash needed Selina's help. Her hands grazed his body on two separate occasions, sending little charges up her arms. She set these aside, problems for another day.

Finally, they were ready. A full kilometer each of anchored nanotube rope to hold them up, climbing hooks attached to their harnesses in case they encountered a problem with the rope system. She gave Gash a brief tutorial on how to belay, to make sure he had a controlled descent into the pit instead of just careening to his death.

"Should someone be standing guard...?" Frederick asked at the end of this lesson. "I mean, in case the White Lotus come back?"

Selina had thought this, but after what Valkyrie had done, she did not think either group would have the manpower to send back out to the Pit. At least not immediately. Nevertheless, she looked at Gash. Perhaps he'd volunteer for this task rather than risking his life climbing into the deep recesses of the planet. He shook his head, intent on joining her.

And so, an hour after Valkyrie had wiped out both armies and left the path clear for them, mere moments after weeks of digging dovetailed into the perfectly timed completion of the expedition, Selina, Frederick, and Gash stood on the precipice of a kilometer long vertical drop. Was it luck? Was it fate? Things were not as they seemed, Selina perceived this clearly. But none of that mattered now. Unknown mysteries called from the deep.

She jumped.

GASH

Gash fell through darkness. For a moment the sensation took him utterly, the stale air of the unsealed cave mixed with the ozone of the laser drill in his nose, his senses and his conscious mind disengaged from the reality of the world above. Yes, a part of him knew he had to control his own descent, or he would eventually hit a terminal velocity, breaking his harness if he tried to stop, breaking his harness and falling to the bottom of Selina's pit if he didn't. But for the moment he'd been paralyzed by the memory, a lifetime ago, of meeting Serena.

A jazz club in Seattle, filled with smoke. Vending machines lined a far wall, churning out cigarettes and recreational drugs by the fistful. The other wall had been plastered with slot machines – gambling had come back into vogue a few years earlier, and the damn things were everywhere. In between, a dark room and tables full of people wearing the year's latest trends in synth-leather, the stage on the far side of the club dark and empty, the jazz being piped in from a digital radio station. Live music slated for later.

"Gash!"

How far away Selina's voice sounded brought Gash back around and he squeezed the grip for the climbing cable, put the brakes on, just like she'd showed him, the cable going sideways and creating friction with the pulley attached to the harness. The soft mesh grip dug into his hand, and it took several meters for him to stop, the harness digging into his flesh and shuddering his bones. He swung into the side of the hole, the hard rock biting his shoulder.

He held in place for a moment, watching Selina and Frederick sliding towards him from above, the light of the tent above already shrunken to the size of the moon. They took little frog hops. He studied them as they went.

Finally, they both reached him, Selina's face a portrait of concern and anger. When she spoke again it was the tone of voice his mother had used, decades ago.

"Are you trying to get yourself killed? Why use the equipment at all?"

"Sorry," Gash said. "I guess the moment took me. I'm good now."

Frederick said something in a rye tone of voice, but Gash had already begun to descend again, long drops, relishing the sensation of motion, the air rushing past.

He'd followed her to the jazz club as part of a job. She was the job, in fact. His bread and butter, a jealous spouse convinced that there was an affair. He'd seen pictures of Serena first, of course. Young, compared to the husband. Gash was younger, then, too. He'd heard this story before; the older husband convinced himself that his beautiful wife was stepping out on him and hired someone to prove it, for the divorce settlement and for the satisfaction of being right. Was she actually cheating? These things were about 50/50.

Serena, it seemed, would be on the cheating side of 50, having called her husband to let him know she would be stuck working a double (she was a nurse) moments before stepping out into the night air outside the hospital and catching a cab. Gash, camped outside of the hospital with a cell phone tracker programmed into the GPS computer of his old Toyota, followed at a distance until the cab stopped and let her out at the jazz club. A great place for meeting a lover or finding a new one.

He parked in a nearby lot, the scanner charging his cred-stick remotely and sending a receipt to his email that would be forwarded directly to a folder titled "Expenses." When he stepped into the club, the music and the smoke and the muffled roar of quiet conversation multiplied across many tables all hit him in a wall. When he saw Serena sitting alone at the bar, his heartbeat picked up a couple of paces. She wasn't particularly dressed up, nondescript slacks and a long non-branded shirt. But something about her accelerated his breathing and got him to thinking thoughts he shouldn't be thinking. Especially not on a job like this.

Selina spoke, jarring Gash loose from the memory. "No kidding," Frederick responded.

Gash had started to feel something; not sleepy, exactly, but hypnotized by the rhythmic motion and the darkness of the descent. As though on cue, Selina flipped on the LED light on her climbing harness. Frederick followed suit. Gash realized he had one of these as well and did the same. Figured he better pay attention to where he was going. It did not take long for his mind to return to the memory from here.

Gash had taken a table at the back of the club, sliding a cigarette out of the pack he kept in his jacket pocket. The smoke filled his lungs, coating his insides and slowing the pounding of his heart. He watched Serena order a drink at the bar. It didn't take more than two minutes for the guy to show up. Tall, with taste in clothes somehow both expensive and terrible.

Only this wasn't "the guy." It was some random guy, hitting on her, and she turned him away with a shake of the head. Odd. After taking a sip of her drink, she stepped away from the bar and went towards the far wall vending machines. Stood in front of the WalCo one, and plugged her cred-stick in. Tapped a few buttons, before bending down to withdraw something from the machine and then returning to her seat. She ripped a little package open and dropped two tablets into her drink. The drink fizzed a little bit, and she took a big long pull.

Some kind of recreational pharmaceuticals. Pharmas like that, dispensed by WalCo and dropped into beverages, were generally in the family of mood-alterers. Addicting, but with fairly modest effects on the user. When she'd had three drinks with three packets of the drugs within an hour, spurning twice as many advances from random men (and one woman), Gash had a vision – a vision of his "expenses" folder dissolving into the digital ether, of an angry client with red eyes raging at him. None of that mattered anymore, Serena didn't need a meddling husband, she needed him to save her. Before he got up, before he sat beside her, before he looked her in the eye and told her that her husband had hired him to follow her, he sat there in the club watching her. His heart swelled, choking the breath out of him. If there was one thing Nagash Jensen could be counted on to do, it was to fall hard and fall fast.

How long had they been descending? When Gash looked up, he couldn't see the entrance through which they'd descended, only the harsh white lights on Selina and Frederick's harnesses. Below, of course, only darkness. He tried to angle his chest downwards, to focus the beam of the light towards the bottom but couldn't make the contortion. He simply continued to descend then, his entire reality composed of his two companions above and the narrow cylinder of light immediately around him, his LED illuminating the too-smooth walls of black rock.

After a time, without any kind of warning, Gash realized that the cylinder of light was no longer a cylinder. He'd passed through the lasered-out tunnel and into the Pit. Much to his surprise, he found himself standing on stairs made of stone, about two feet wide, carved into the side of the Pit. He turned around, trying to get his bearings, and could feel a strange sensation building in the bottom of his stomach. A sensation of largeness. He shone his light along the stairs. They wound down in one direction, and up in the other. Only by following them with his light did he realize the scope of the Pit. It was massive – cavern seemed more appropriate than pit, now that he found himself down here – and though he couldn't see the full size in the darkness, he felt dizzy from the realization of scale.

And beyond that, what the hell would any of them make of something like this? Selina said it had to be a naturally occurring phenomenon of some kind. It was buried a full kilometer under the surface of the island of Rhodes, but it had stairs carved into the side? That ruled out natural phenomenon, but who could have undertaken such a project, and how long ago must it have happened? Who could have achieved this in ancient times, and how had they gotten out, and why? And what lay at the bottom of those stairs? And why weren't there *railings*?

Selina appeared from the hole above and into the Pit, landing on the stairs beside him. The sharp intake of breath, and her whispered words – *holy hell* – seemed to echo back up to the surface and down into the Pit below, reverberating endlessly. He took a deep breath and looked at her, his next words at the tip of his tongue: "What now?"

SAGE

When Sage and Hiro returned to the castle, they found the twin doors standing ajar, the walls above empty. Hiro didn't need to say "I told you so," merely letting his faint smile do the work for him. Sage rolled their eyes and the two stepped into the courtyard.

The place had been beautifully landscaped, Sage mused. Not bad for a secret organization of historically themed murderers who had taken over an entire island. Lilies and creeping vines and what looked like olive plants grew in over-abundance in the green space between the outside world and the castle's interior doors. The irrigation costs would have been extensive. No time to enjoy the garden, however. Hiro led the way into the castle proper.

Sage shut the door behind them, the sudden drop in ambient light casting everything into shadow. They walked past old suits of armor, olive branches hanging above each, some symbolism that Sage did not have time to analyze. Hiro's demeanor told Sage that he knew where he was going, and he was eager to get there – that was wrong. He shouldn't have any better idea than Sage about where to go. But what to do about it? Hiro had done nothing untrustworthy since the two had partnered up; on the contrary, he'd been the most faithful partner they had ever been assigned by Interpol.

The silence weighed on Sage as they passed through another door, entering a large courtyard with marbled floors. Sage, having just grown used to the dim interior, squinted at the blast of fresh sunlight. White statues lined the courtyard, one per archway, as they passed through and back into an interior space on the other side. Here, Sage grabbed Hiro by the shoulder and stopped him.

He turned to look at them. "What is it, partner?"

"What the hell is going on? You obviously know exactly where you're going, and you knew that nobody would be home. Explain."

Hiro seemed to consider their words for a moment. "All will be answered shortly. I'm just going to ask you to trust me for now."

"That's not good enough," Sage said.

"You can turn around and leave the way we came in if you prefer," he said.

Sage and Hiro both knew that they would not be able to do any such thing. So, without further words, they followed. Whatever happened, happened. Sage had come too far, given up too much, to balk at the end. Whatever the end was.

It came quickly, or its beginning did. Hiro led them through one more door at the end a long hallway. Sage found themself inside a medium sized room. A white chandelier hung above and carved into the white stone of the wall stood a mighty fireplace, long empty, flanked by two marble pillars. Near the far wall, a table with four chairs faced the entryway from across the room.

Three of the men, Sage didn't recognize. They wore red cloaks of course, as all their counterparts, but these men were older. The white of what wispy hair remained on their heads or faces matched the white of the marble columns. They sat with dignity, staring at Sage and Hiro.

The fourth man, Sage recognized. Gerard.

"I killed you," Sage said.

"You did, yes," Gerard said. "Almost. If you only knew what I had

—

inside me, you might have hit me a few extra times with that coward's weapon of yours. Even my auxiliary life support organs wouldn't have been able to handle the extra trauma."

"Your pulse," Sage started.

"Was undetectable while some of my extras kept just enough blood pumping to my vital organs to extend my life until my associates could come for me. Don't you think it's important to be the best you that you can be? Do you have any enhancements, Agent Menotti? Or are you more like your White Lotus compatriot?"

Sage caught Hiro's eyes, and they said what they needed to. He really *was* White Lotus. That would explain how he knew where to find Gerard. If they were at war, and Sage was just a pawn, was this the final showdown between leaders?

"Yes," Gerard said, "I must admit I was surprised to hear that you had partnered with the Grand Teacher of the Japanese branch of the White Lotus."

He rose to his feet without warning. Sage's weapons were unholstered and pointed at the man before he could push his chair in. He raised his hands halfway, a sad little smile on his face.

"No need for that, Agent Menotti. I know when I've been beaten. The clever alliance between the White Lotus and the Children of Gaia proved to be more than we could handle. Between the two of you and that mechanized mercenary that the Children deployed, our numbers are devastated. We have lost."

"Though I think you do not know the stakes, do you, Agent?"

"What are you talking about, Gerard? What stakes? I'm just here to bring about justice, an end to your little secret war."

Gerard laughed, once. "I was not born Gerard, you know. I took this name and cast aside the name of my birth. Blessed Gerard founded our order over 1000 years ago. Originally the Knights Hospitaller existed to protect Christian pilgrims in the Holy Land at the Hospital of St. John.

"But that all changed after the fall of Jerusalem. Our order fled to Rhodes, where we made a startling discovery. Magic, a force known to the holy and unholy in the 11th century, did not exist in the world without source. We found the source – or a source, anyway – at the bottom of a massive pit, far beneath this island. Local magicians, geomancers they were known as, called upon the power of the Earth to build their towns, bring rain for their crops, to kill each other. Magic, long a font of strife in the world, flourished on the Island of Rhodes. Magic had toppled one of the ancient wonders of the world, the great Colossus of Rhodes, centuries earlier.

"The people were sick of it, sick of watching those with greater power tear down what they had built. Our order changed its name to the Knights of Rhodes and dedicated itself to finding a way to remove the blight of magic from the world. After all, who needs magic when you have the Will of God?"

"This is crazy," Sage said. "I'm taking you back with me to Interpol. I don't have time to stand here and listen to your ramblings."

"But don't you see? This is why my Knights have fought Hiro's White Lotus for centuries. They discovered what we did. Isn't that right, Hiroyuki?"

Hiro watched Sage for a moment before responding. "I would like to say, Sage, that I am no longer of the Order of the White Lotus. I split from the leadership, on account of a difference in philosophy."

"So, you're not going to agree with me that all talk of magic is bullshit? Not going to deny that you're White Lotus?" Sage asked, one of their guns migrating, until they found it pointed at Hiro.

Hiro laughed, long and rich and hearty, his chest heaving. "I told you once. I have lived many lives before. Kings and peasants, warriors more times than I might have hoped. And yes, magicians from the time when such things were still possible. The White Lotus formed because magic is not the evil blight that this man and his ilk believe it to be. For millennia my people: the Japanese, the Koreans, the Chinese, the Vietnamese; all used magic for good. To control the flow of chi in the body, we could heal most any ailment. Ritual magic could be channeled to bring about bountiful harvest. The people of Rhodes did this as well, before the Knights took it away."

"Oh please," Gerard snorted. "We both know that magic killed as many or more than it saved. We have books upon books detailing the tragedies caused by magic through the original eras. Texts from Ancient Greece to Persia speak of strix, blood drinking demons. Christians have battled against possessions by magical entities since Christ first showed us a way to banish them. Even China saw countless deaths from magic users. Take, for instance, the famous mystic who rebelled against the Han empire 800 years before the formation of our order. The Yellow Turban rebellion, a peasant uprising, was in truth an attempt by a powerful magic user to take control of an entire nation using his powers. How many died because one man received great power by chance and chose to misuse it?"

"It doesn't matter." Hiro said. "Your people had no right to so drastically devastate the natural order of things. They were poisoned by a sense of patriarchal duty to the world, some notion that a small handful of men knew what was best for all. Or perhaps they simply did not know the scope of the atrocity that they would commit?"

"What atrocity? What did the Knights do?" Sage asked. Their arms were growing tired, but still they kept the weapons pointed at the two men, Gerard and Hiro. It was the only control they could muster, as an impossible story unfolded in front of them. Something that could not be true, but yet, had a ring of truth in some primal place deep in Sage's heart.

"We saved the world from itself," Gerard said.

"They set the world on a path of slow destruction, humanity falling out of touch with the natural world and beginning to destroy it for short-sighted personal gain."

"We set humanity free to flourish as a species, and the tale is the greatest epic of heroism to go unrecorded in public history books. Eventually, after much study, the Knights formulated a plan. The source of magic beneath the island of Rhodes was known to exist deep in the earth, its occasional outgassing of energy having exposed it to the world. Powerful enchanters carved stone steps down to the source, so they could draw power from it directly.

"We had also learned that copper disrupted the flow of magical energies. So, the Knights of Rhodes forged a mighty copper greatsword. A champion was chosen, a great knight who had taken the name of the founder, just as I have. Blessed Gerard took the copper sword and travelled alone down to the source. Once down there, a handful of geomancers loyal to our cause closed the hole from above using their magic.

"Having been buried deep beneath the surface, Blessed Gerard plunged the copper sword into the fabric of the source. As the elders had expected, humanity ceased to have access to the magical energies they had for centuries misused on each other. And, the flow of magic having been stopped, the source could not be accessed to undo the work. Blessed Gerard died a slow death, we suspect, though we cannot know. What we know is that he sacrificed himself to make the world a better place, and for centuries we have tried to keep secret and protect our work."

"That's a hell of a tall tale," Sage said.

"All true, but for the little ideological embellishments," Hiro said.

"Well, thanks for sharing it. Now I think I'm bringing you both in."

"Don't you understand?" Gerard said. "Hiro's puppets are about to undo our work. Can you imagine what will happen when magic floods back into this world after a thousand years? Vampires running amok? Were-creatures? Men who can open holes in the earth or create and manipulate fire at will? You can help stop this before it's too late."

"First of all, they are not my puppets," Hiro said. "When it became clear that the White Lotus wanted to find a way to secretly bottle the source and use it to further its own power, I realized that the order I had served for many lives had finally become as corrupted as the Knights of Rhodes. But there was another, called the Children of Gaia. I have helped them in my own small ways for the last few years. They, like I, believe that magic is the birthright of the human race. And we are restoring that birthright even now. Our agent will not fail, and there would not be time for Sage to stop him, even if they felt so inclined."

"That's it," Sage said. "All of you get in the corner. I'm calling Interpol."

FREDERICK

Shallow, controlled breaths. Don't give anything away. His whole life, Frederick had been working towards this. The Speaker had cultivated him from birth as surely as he had directed Selina from afar, guiding them both towards their fate from infancy. It would not do to give away the game now, in the hour of triumph.

Frederick followed Selina and Gash as they stepped carefully down a pathway carved in stone by ancient geomancers many centuries ago.

He did not mind these two, and his heart quailed at the thought of his own betrayal. His own life had been forfeit to this cause since birth, but they had no inkling of what they had stumbled into. Still, the cause reached far beyond them, and he could give them no greater thought than this: Perhaps they would live.

When Selina stumbled, Gash reached out to steady her. It was the perfect moment to strike. He saw it in his mind's eye first. One step down to their step, and then his hands outreached as his two erstwhile companions plunged to their deaths far below. His instructions were clear: eliminate Selina and Gash so he could

—

complete his mission alone, with no chance of failure. The look on Selina's face rattled him. Of hurt, of terrified betrayal, of frustration at getting so close only to lose it all. She plunged so slowly to her death that he had hours to watch that look on her face.

He couldn't do it. Could not deny them the glory of discovery in their final moments. He remained on his step until Selina found her balance again, and then continued to hike down behind them.

Down they travelled, the silence of their passage dwarfed by the roaring silence of a space so vast, buried for so long, beneath so much rock. The silence here truly echoed. Three beams of light cutting through Magic's tomb marked the first sign of life in this space for over a thousand years. In each beam could be seen curling dust, rising in thin spirals through the dead air towards the fresh opening countless meters above.

When Selina stopped short many hours into their trek, Frederick knew they were near. She gave a sharp gasp, and he craned to see what she saw. A small coin of light, far below them. Not the harsh light of the sun or the warm light of molten rock, but a soft blue, cool and inviting, gradually shifting spectrum to green, then yellow, and then red. A tiny prism far below them.

The Source.

SELINA

With each step, the truth revealed itself by centimeters. The light below proved to be neither an artificial source of light, nor a known source of natural light. They had stumbled onto something undiscovered in modern times. The whole floor of the pit flickered and undulated, impossible to identify exactly as a liquid or solid. And with each footfall bringing her closer, Selina's fingers tingled a little more. She felt a sort of energy stir inside her.

She wanted to imagine scientifically plausible explanations. The problem was, there were none. In the category of scientifically implausible, but maybe possible; she imagined an alien craft of some sort, crashed eons ago, its power source still functional. But that wouldn't explain stone steps carved in a great spiral around the impact cavity, nor would it explain the lack of a crater at the surface. The physics of the situation didn't fit in with that theory.

Selina could see the writing on the wall. All the talk about magic, she'd mostly ignored it. But how else could she begin to understand what was resolving beneath her as she climbed down?

How long had they climbed? Hours, certainly. Two? Four? Ten?

Time had lost all meaning, and Selina had not felt even a trace of exhaustion or pain. Only drive, only an elation deep in her heart that came from something primal inside.

When they were close – maybe twenty stories above the pit's floor – a sense of vertigo overwhelmed her, and Selina staggered backwards, taking a seat to avoid falling to her death. When she closed her eyes to see if that would help, something fantastical happened. As her eyes closed, a vision struck her, as though a second pair of eyes in another dimension or reality had opened.

A group of four red-cloaked men stood around the guillotine in the wood-paneled room. The room looked much the same as when Selina found it, except the guillotine was intact. And a man kneeled before it, his head locked in place beneath the blade. The men spoke amongst themselves, quietly. The man closed his eyes, shouted something in French, and then the nearest of the Knights reached out to flip a lever. The guillotine's blade dropped, severing the Frenchman's head from his body. The body slumped, and the disembodied head landed in a small basket at the foot of the guillotine.

Somehow Selina knew: This was the past. Moreover, she could tell that the executed man had been Rembert. Which explained why his journal had never been finished, why his story had never been completed and the foot of the Colossus never returned. She knew it with the same certainty provided by a dream, except that this wasn't a dream. Not quite. Selina could still hear Gash and Frederick talking to her, somewhere on another plane of existence.

Magic. There could be no other explanation, and her heart knew it. This vision, a symptom of her proximity to this strange font of magical energy, was from the past. And more than that, Selina could *feel* her second set of eyes. Could use them to look around, somehow.

This journey had moved beyond the Colossus of Rhodes, but it had started there. Selina Kan's favorite pastime was always sitting with her father, speculating about what really happened to the Colossus. Now, forces beyond her understanding had given her a window into the past. She concentrated on going further. On the distant past.

Mounted on a breakwater in the harbor of the ancient city of Rhodes stood a mighty bronze statue, which, not unlike another great colossus, held a torch aloft to the sky. Helios, god of the sun. Celebration of freedom for the people of Rhodes, who vanquished Demetrius and his armies. The sun god stood proudly, his other hand clutching a cloak over his left shoulder.

Around this Colossus swarmed several dozen boats, small Greek galleys. Battle frothed the waters of the harbor of Rhodes. Men in black cloaks stood on the bow of each ship, executing arcane gestures. From these erupted what could only be described as magical attacks. One threw a great ball of fire at a neighboring ship, the timber and sails igniting immediately, men leaping, burning, into the water. From another ship came a great surge of water, washing over the deck of the first, sending the fire-wielding mage into the sea beside his victims, splitting his ship in two.

The battle carried on, as balls of fire, gouts of water, and surging bolts of electricity flew freely about the harbor. Errant flashes of magical power flew by the dozens, striking at the infrastructure on the shore, and fire began to creep up the streets from the harbor. Buildings burned and collapsed, ships sank, and men cried their deaths. And then someone new appeared. On the docks he stood, a voluminous white robe obscuring his features. He raised both hands, and stood like that for a moment, unnoticed by the two naval forces. And then he fell to his knees, and a cone of white-blue light erupted from his fingers. It swept the harbor, incinerating every ship, every battling mage disappearing in a flash of destruction.

The wave hit the Colossus, too, searing through its ankles. It did not topple immediately. For an instant after the light disappeared, it seemed as though the world had already forgotten the battle. Boats sank into the harbor and survivors began the swim to shore. And only then, when it was truly ready, did the Colossus of Rhodes topple backwards onto an outcropping of land beside the breakwater, shattering as it struck the earth.

Incredible. Selina opened her eyes. Gash and Frederick looked as though they were about to come to blows. As soon as she stirred, the argument stopped. Gash knelt by her.

"What was that? Are you okay? Do we need to go back? Do you need some water?"

She reached out, placing two fingers on his lips. "I'm fine. I just… well, I think I just had a vision of the past. It was incredible. I don't really know how to process it yet, but I'll tell you all about it later."

"A vision?" Frederick said. "That's incredible!"

"Magic, huh?" Gash said.

Selina nodded.

"I guess at this point, I can't roll my eyes anymore."

"We're almost there," Frederick said.

So, they pressed on. Selina felt woozy still, but pushed through it, walking the last steps as though in a dream. The last stone slab protruded from the wall of the Pit about half a meter above the shimmering, polychromatic floor. Selina paused above it, the archaeologist inside taking over. How best to sample the floor? It would be paramount to figure out if the surface could be walked on safely. It gave off no heat, so that was a good start. But would they sink into it? Would it react violently to their footfalls? What the hell *was* it? How the hell did one excavate a magical hole in the ground?

Before Selina could resolve any of the questions in her head, Frederick barreled past.

"Fred, hang on!" Gash said, reaching too late to stop the young man.

His feet hit the floor hard, and he stood for a second, grinning chaotically. "The Source," he said. "We've found it after 700 years. Do you have any idea what this means? You've begun to have an inkling, but you can't know the full extent of it. Soon you will." He turned away before she could say anything and began moving towards the center of the space.

Only then did Selina see what appeared to be a large two-handed sword, buried almost to the hilt in the center of the prismatic surface. The light flickered around it, a small dim spot immediately around the blade that looked, somehow, like a festering wound in reality itself. In the wash of soft light, shifting colors every few moments, Selina had trouble identifying many details. It definitely dated from the 14th or 15th century, if the hiltwork were to be believed. But the material looked wrong. Bronze? Copper? Nothing anyone normally used to craft a weapon during that era. Maybe up close she could identify more. Frederick was making his way across the surface towards the blade, fast. Something was wrong. Evidently Gash could feel it too. He pulled out his gun and pointed it at Frederick.

"Wait," Selina said, placing her hand on Gash's, lowering the firearm. "Let me talk to him."

He said nothing but did not raise the weapon a second time.

"Frederick, what are you doing?" Selina called out.

He did not turn around. "Restoring Mother Earth to her natural state."

"It's obvious you weren't truthful with us when you signed on, but that's okay. None of us was totally honest. Come back here and let's talk calmly about this," Selina said, trailing off at the end. He was almost to the sword and showing no sign of slowing down. Had she made the right decision? Should she have let Gash shoot him? It was too late now, he was reaching for the blade.

"This is for Mothe –" he started to say but did not have the chance to finish. The instant his fingers closed around the hilt of the sword, his head rocked back, and a blinding white light erupted from his mouth, rising in a tight beam into the darkness above.

And then with a great heave, Frederick pulled the sword loose. From the freshly opened wound in what he had called the Source, a much wider pillar of light exploded upwards. It consumed Frederick and the sword, disintegrating them in a flash similar to what toppled the Colossus in Selina's vision.

The Source seemed to be coming to life, flowing in and around itself, waves of light strobing out from the center in concentric circles. And then the larger pillar of light pulsated once, twice, and a booming shockwave threw her into the wall. Far above, a sister shockwave reverberated back down towards Selina and Gash. The thick layer of earth, a kilometer above, being blasted away by the sudden surge of energy. Selina couldn't see it yet, but she could hear it – a stone avalanche. Thousands of tons of dirt and clay cascading down into the Pit. The world was collapsing on them.

Selina's body buzzed. Somewhere far away, she felt pain. But as she recovered her balance, she came to realize that her neurons were firing in a way completely foreign to her. If she had a second pair of eyes when she had her dream-like vision, she now had a second muscular system in her body, separate but not unlike the one she'd grown up with. She tried flexing one of these muscles and blue light burst from her fingertips.

She looked at Gash. He stared at her. No, through her. Like he hadn't even seen what she'd just done. And his eyes – were they red now? It was hard to say with all the flashing lights that bathed them. He took one step toward her, arm outstretched, and then a step away. After a last moment's hesitation, he turned and ran up the stairs.

And he was fast. So fast. No human, Selina knew, had ever run so fast. He was above her in seconds, covering hundreds of steps in an instant.

That was when she saw the debris. Huge boulders and great clumps of earth crashing towards her from above, careening back and forth within the confines of the Pit's walls. She had only a second to prepare herself for death as a vertical landslide roared towards her, smashing chunks out of the walls above.

In the final heartbeat before the collapsing debris buried her, Selina's new "muscles" tensed as though of their own accord, and her arms flashed up and before she could even register the movements of her own body, a translucent blue dome materialized two meters above her head. Giant boulders struck it and were popped like balloons, the thick dust of them propelled directly sideways, and falling around her in a pile with the rest of the debris that had not struck the dome.

When the dust settled, Selina found herself standing in a hole, three or four meters in diameter that reached above her head. She had survived, somehow. When she relaxed, the dome disappeared. She climbed out of the hole and surveyed the area. The stairs had been demolished. She looked up and around but saw no sign of Gash.

—

Had he been pulverized in the cave-in? She somehow suspected he had not, though she couldn't say why.

But now she was trapped. She couldn't climb out of a pit of this depth, and with the climbing gear she'd brought down, it was unlikely she'd have the strength to get all the way to the top.

Before despair could set in, she made one last discovery, there in the bottom of the pit. She could float. Again, her new muscles were moving on their own – was this her subconscious? This time she rose gently into the air, as though riding an invisible elevator.

She would, she understood, float directly up and out of this pit under no power that she recognized as of this world. Something had changed in her, fundamentally. She had magic. And that feeling was in no way limited to her immediate person. It permeated everything. The rocks, the air, her distant impressions of the world far above. Magic. Alive in the world again, as though it had always been this way.

She ascended on a force of strange energy, up from the stale cavern and into the starry night above, a million twinkling points of light calling to her like they'd never done before.

EPILOGUE – SAGE

When Sage awoke inside a tiny apartment, their brain worked sluggishly to come to life. Their mouth felt dry and cracked, their limbs heavy as though from an extended sleep. They sat up and looked out the window at a massive city. Dark night sky and bright lights warred in cloud-scrapers above, and the sprawl below twinkled endlessly, ten billion street lights and headlights and night lights and neon lights. Infinite light above and below, but in the tiny apartment, darkness. Beside the bed, on a small nightstand, stood a tall glass of water. With their right hand, Sage grabbed it and took a tender sip, and then another, the parched flesh in the back of their throat absorbing it greedily.

With a soft flick, a dim light came to life in the ceiling above. Sage turned in the bed to see Hiro entering the small room with two cartons of noodles. He sat on the other single bed beside Sage's, and offered a carton of noodles.

Hiro's face ushered in a flood of memory.

Interpol had come, when Sage had called. They had let command know the whole thing, that they had Gerard in custody and a high

ranking member of the White Lotus who had infiltrated Interpol.
Command had acknowledged.

Several hours later, Sage sitting at Gerard's old seat, the
prisoners huddled in the corner, two Interpol agents had arrived.
Only two. One team, and more specifically, a team of two that had
tried multiple times to take over the Gerard case when Sage had
faltered. Agents Stoddard and Bruneau.

Stoddard looked from Sage to Gerard, and back to Sage, and said
"We're here, Grandmaster."

Before Sage could register it fully, Stoddard had drawn on them,
his black pistol roaring, the gunpowder of it filling their ears even as
the force of impact knocked them backwards to the floor.

Their shoulder smoldered. It roared, the heat of it spreading to
neighboring limbs and organs. When Sage had looked over at it, they
saw blood. Lots of it. Stoddard stood over them, and they could hear
Hiro scuffling with Bruneau, Gerard, and the elders. Stoddard shook
his head in mock sorrow, a grin plastered across his idiot face. Faster
than they imagined possible, Sage had pulled a second gauss pistol
from the holster at their hip and put two in Stoddard's chest. He
staggered backwards, dead before he fell, and then Sage had blacked
out.

An explosion outside drew them back to the present. They looked
at Hiro, the question unspoken but not unheard.

"It is war on the streets each night, now. With magic returning to
the world, criminals have new power over police. Corporations
scramble frantically to find new magical assets, trying to get a leg up
over each other by finding the next thrower of fireballs, the next
ancient sword awakened after centuries in a museum somewhere.
Battered wives electrocute their husbands. Your secret war has
multiplied. Now there are a thousand secret wars that begin fresh
each night."

"Did you kill Gerard?"

Hiro shook his head.

"Bruneau?"

"He gave his life for his master to slip out. I could have pursued, but I chose instead to take you to safety."

"We're obviously not in Rhodes anymore."

"Hong Kong," Hiro replied. "That pilot actually waited for us, after all." When he offered the carton of noodles a second time, Sage recognized a great hunger within their belly. They must have been out for days. The glass of water still in their right hand, Sage reached out with their left, only to realize that it was gone. Amputated at the shoulder.

Hiro must have recognized the look on their face, or perhaps had just been planning this moment since the amputation. "I know a guy with top of the line prosthetics, and he owes me a favor. You'll have something better than the original within the week."

Sage felt a faint seed of panic inside, but it did not blossom. Instead, they felt only a sense of inner peace. Why? Gerard had gotten away, and Sage could never return to Interpol. As far as command would be concerned, they'd sent two legitimate agents to rein in two rogue agents, and the legitimate team was now dead. Unless Interpol HQ was in on it from the start, they would never believe Sage's and Hiro's story. Sage now floated adrift from their life plan, unemployed, armless, and a failure. So why the sense of inner peace?

"You are wondering what that serenity is, inside of you?"

"Are you literally reading my mind?"

Hiro laughed, setting both cartons of noodles on the nightstand, and rising to walk to the window. "I have told you that I remember each of my lives. I have told you that I have lived as beggar, as king, as warrior, as many different things. But what I haven't told you is that in every one of my lives I have been a healer, able to channel the flow of chi within the body to the benefit of my patient. At least until the Knights of Rhodes."

"And that has what to do with my amputated arm and sense of unlikely well-being?"

"The chi within you has never been properly directed. For centuries, only a few of the most well-disciplined minds in the world could direct even their own body's chi. But now magic has returned to the world. When the body is in balance, it does not matter if a limb is missing or if one has failed, because with balance comes harmony, and with harmony comes peace."

"Hiro, you sound like a fortune cookie."

Hiro laughed, turning from the window. "And yet you cannot deny how you feel. In time you will come to believe me, and you will learn the stories of each of my lives. For now, however, you will need to learn to eat noodles one handed, and then get some more rest. Tomorrow we're going arm shopping."

EPILOGUE – SELINA

When Selina stepped back into her home after being gone for weeks, the smell of stale pizza boxes hit her in a tidal wave. She keyed the security code into the terminal on the wall beside the door, and the maglocks slid into place. Flipped the two manual deadbolts into place as well. Humidity had crept in after a couple weeks of low-AC usage. She cranked the thermostat down to 80 and the system clattered to life.

For a moment, she stood in the middle of the apartment, taking in the dank musk beneath the smell of residual pizza. The thick coating of dust. The walls sweating with the Jacksonville moisture that permeated everything. It all felt different now. Was it because she had magic? She had seen the past, annihilated an avalanche of falling boulders, and floated out of a hole deep beneath the Earth. She had flown all the way across the Island of Rhodes to the airstrip and caught a ride on a shuttle with the two Interpol agents before she faltered. She had ridden with Hiro and the other one, Sage, who'd been wounded in a battle with the Knights, to Hong Kong. From there, the shuttle pilot had taken them both back to Jacksonville.

Did this new feeling arise from her new powers then? Or was it because she had discovered the real story of the Colossus of Rhodes, now knew the location of a missing piece of the mighty statue, a fact that would surely be a foot in the door to her childhood dream of becoming an archaeologist? Forget a foot in the door, that discovery alone would be a full passage through the door to the other side. But she'd have to act quickly. The blogosphere buzzed with reports of Valkyrie in Rhodes, with an explosion of light seen in Rhodes, with a woman seen flying through the air as if by magic in Rhodes. It hadn't taken any geniuses to connect these reports with the fact that magic had swept back into the world at the same time that the explosion had occurred. Rhodes would be a *very* different place when she returned, swarming with corporate teams trying to harness the Source for maximum profit. She had pictures of the foot, and coordinates for the ancient temple, which would hopefully remain safe until her imminent return.

Her rig blinked with a new message. That would be the Smithsonian responding to her message, finally. She'd been keeping on her emails with her PCom while she travelled but hadn't checked in a few hours. The gene scan whirred, and when it verified that she was herself, booted up. Within a few seconds, she had plugged into the jack behind her left ear and was diving through the artificial astro-scape that served as her OS.

The email had NOT come from the Smithsonian. It was a short note from a throwaway URL.

Selina, I know you have unresolved business in Rhodes, and I know it's time-sensitive. But I have to tell you that I think we were both used by the same organization to bring about this return of magic to the world. The thousands of people dying, the countless skirmishes, we can trace these all back to an organization called the Children of Gaia.

I did some research. Your father was a member. I was impressed by you in our brief meeting, and I'd like to team up on getting some

V for Valkyrie? It had to be. Selina let the email spin out into the darkness. If her neurons had not all been tied into the motions of her avatar through the void of cyberspace, she would have rocked back in her chair. Her father, a member of a secret organization devoted to the return of magic to the world? There was no way. He'd been a simple man who loved his daughter. Why lie to her?

But then, why would Valkyrie lie about something like that? A billionaire mercenary that lived in outer space did NOT have a motive for telling such a specific lie. Selina did want answers: The idea that she'd been used, been secretly groomed towards this end since childhood, festered deep within her.

But Rhodes couldn't wait. The Colossus couldn't wait. And she couldn't wait for the Smithsonian to get around to reading her messages. Probably they just thought she was a quack.

She would get a crew from Hemmingway. He seemed to have a thing for helping her, and there would be plenty of money in a discovery like this. She chartered a heavy-duty shuttle that could haul something as heavy as the Foot of the Colossus and fired off a request for a meet with Hemmingway.

At last, her dreams were within her reach, but she would have to reach out fast to seize them. Then, somewhere along the way, she'd have to figure out what exactly had happened down beneath the surface of the Earth. She'd have to figure out what it meant to have magical powers, and what had become of Nagash Jensen, her faithful bodyguard.

EPILOGUE – GASH

When the wall of energy had thrown him into the stone wall of the pit, a hunger had descended upon Gash like none other he'd ever experienced. He had smelled it pumping in Selina's throat – like before but a hundred times more vividly. Now he tasted the heat of it just beneath the surface of her skin. It had required every ounce of his will to turn away. When he found himself climbing the broken stone walls like a spider, the earth crashing past him but somehow not crushing him, Gash had very little mental capacity for doing anything but holding back the hunger. A distant part of him thought of her being crushed beneath the rocks, but he could do nothing to save her. Could do nothing but get as far away as fast as possible before he lost control and did something to her himself.

At the surface, under the faint light of stars, he found that he could see *everything*, as well as he ever had during any day in the sun. The night blurred in his memory, but Gash did remember later in the night, a mugger finding him in an alley in Rhodes. Gash had swatted the man's knife away and lifted him from the ground, before ripping his throat out and drinking deeply of the man's arterial blood as it pumped and sprayed from his body. Gash drank and drank, as the ebb slowed, and the man drooped. Not until the flow had stopped did Gash discard the body.

Then, drenched in human blood and able to think clearly for the first time since his transformation, Gash began to panic. He was a *vampire* of all things. Real life, just like the movies (well, not the teen movies, but the *old* movies).

In the morning he had tried his luck with the sun, and less than a full minute in its blinding embrace had scorched his skin so badly that he could smell the burning. It had taken two days, hidden inside an old abandoned storefront that once sold tourist memorabilia, before he recovered. But he had confirmed it for himself. A *vampire*.

From there, Gash found himself at a loss. Escape from WalCo had been the plan. He was meant to have returned to Florida long enough to get his documents from Hemmingway, and then collect his pay from Selina, and disappear into the sunset. But now he'd run from Selina, who'd in all likelihood returned to the States without him. Alone, halfway around the world from the WalCo HQ, with no money. Not his finest moment, but then, Nagash Jensen could always be counted on to find a way to get what he needed. Or something approximating it. Where would he go?

Steal a boat, that would be the first plan. The marina nearby had seen better days. Five or six fishing boats floated in their berths, chipped paint and second-hand electronics equipment from the previous decades mounted on the rooftops. One ship, though, stood out. A brand new yacht rested in the spot furthest from the shore. As Gash approached it, he could make out the boat's name. "The Holy."

Had to be the Hospitallers. The Knights of Rhodes. Whoever. They had been the only ones with money in these parts. They were pretty much all dead by now anyway, right? So, it was barely even stealing. Gash stepped aboard. It had to be close to thirty feet, meant to be crewed by several people. But something this advanced, he knew, would have a central virtual intelligence that could automate everything. Just had to get logged in on the computer and hope it wasn't password protected. He clambered up to the captain's nest above the crew quarters and pushed the "on" button for the ship's onboard computer.

The seal of the Knights of Rhodes. User name and password. Of course. He looked around for pictures of family members or pets, bits of paper with clues or even the password itself. Tricks that had often worked for him as a P.I., back in the day. But unfortunately, this ship's captain had left nothing of himself. Gash tried his luck with some random usernames and passwords, but naturally found no success. Despair set in and he prepared to give up.

But then the screen went blue, a single blinking white cursor in the top left corner. Words scrolled across the screen.

Hi there, Nagash. I've been watching you ever since you botched the WalCo job I hired you for. I knew you were meant for great things, and I think you're equipped to finish the job now.

Gash cursed. His mystery client back in the day had often communicated like this, hijacking random computer screens to deliver secret messages to him. But he'd given up that job when he'd almost been killed trying to complete it.

I can't hear you if you're saying something but let me suggest that if you'd like to take down payment for resuming the job, this boat might be a good start. I can unlock it for you, program it to take you back to the States. Type "yes" into the password box if you agree to my terms.

Gash took one step back. There were other ways off this island. Plenty of them. But he found himself thinking about the abducted scientist, the old job. The whole case had smelled funny from the start: a client who wouldn't meet face to face, a paycheck that would allow him to retire once and for all, and WalCo. His first impulse had been to say "no" back then, too. But the same thing stopped him then, as now. The abducted woman, a Romanian beauty by the name of Ana Marin, had received a doctorate degree in microbiology by the age of twenty-three. Ten years later, rather than curing the next major designer virus, Ana had disappeared. But her face, blue eyes so bright they were almost white, stared sadly at Gash from the page onto which they had been printed. She needed help, and a beautiful woman in trouble had always been his Achilles' heel.

Nothing had changed since the first time he'd failed. Ana Marin's blue eyes still haunted him, and somewhere on this earth, she still awaited rescue. Everything had changed since the first time he'd failed. He was a bodyguard now – a protector – and yes, some sort of blood drinking monster with super speed and strength.

Nagash Jensen, Private Investigator and newly born vampire, stepped back to the computer screen and pressed down gently on the "Y" key.

Acknowledgements

Unfortunately I have neither the time nor page count to acknowledge every person who has had a hand in helping me grow as a person and therefore a writer. If your name doesn't make it onto this list, please forgive me, and know you have my deepest gratitude for the things or things you did that helped me become the Greg I am in this universe.

First and foremost, I must acknowledge my loving wife, Bailey Ross, who pulled the great bait and switch of 2012 when, on our second date, she gave me incredible edits for a zombie story I was working on, and then proceeded to never give me edits on any of my work ever again. Despite this, you have been incredibly supportive of every great and terrible decision I have made in these last ten years. You are the reason I have not crumbled to dust, given up on everything, or lost my mind. You are the reason I have dogs, for which you deserve all the praise I can muster. Thank you for always being there.

Special thanks, also, to my parents. You have kept me alive for far longer than the parent-child contract traditionally calls for, put me through college and then also paid for my mystifying decision to get an MFA in creative writing. I don't believe I would have the powerful imagination required of a good science fiction writer without your kind and thoughtful parenting. I'm sorry I didn't become an engineer, and I hope that these 85 words make up for any shortfalls in your retirement savings!

I would not feel the pride in *Colossus* that I feel now without the various help of a number of individuals. First and foremost among them, Brandon Getz. Batman, thanks for all the beers, beard-fires, and Resident Evil gaming nights that got me through grad school. "Thanks for your incredible editing skills, as well," he nodded.

Thanks to Nate Ragolia and Shaunn Grulkowski at Spaceboy books for taking a shot on me. And then double thanks for what followed: two years of being digitally henpecked by my needy emails and email follow ups. I think we've made something pretty cool here – thank you for helping me manifest a dream over 20 years in the making!

Thanks, too, to Olivia Croom-Hammerman, AKA the Croom-Hammer (let me know how you feel about your new nickname). I don't know how, but you took my barely-coherent description of what I wanted in a book cover and delivered exactly what I wanted, only better.

A huge thank you is owed to all of my collegiate writing teachers. Across my undergrad and graduate experience, I was extremely fortunate to be able to learn from four incredible fiction instructors. Huge thanks to Jennifer Davis, Teague Bohlen, Sam Ligon, and Gregory Spatz. Each of you patiently humored my sci-fi genre tendencies, and somehow found kernels of competent writing to nurture and grow. Without all four of you, I would no doubt still be writing shameless *Hitchhiker's Guide to the Galaxy* rip offs.

Lastly, I have recently asked for help from friends and family to be early readers for *Colossus*. I was blown away by the number of people that kindly volunteered to read my book ahead of the publication date, in order to be able to able to leave reviews for me right out of the gate. To my friends and my wife's friends: Caitlyn Martin, Cory-Cyone Shaffer, Steven Hanson. To my family or friends of my family: John Ross, Heather Bacani, Molly Jones, Brooke, and Al. To Austin Ross, my friend who is also stuck being my family thanks to his sister's questionable decision. And to all of my new Reddit Friends: VerbalAcrobatics, seanrok, geekandi, nazkar_rikk, FunSizedBear, zer0sum7373, Dont_Order_A_Slayer, wedge713, Toni, Billy, and Jane. I don't know if all of you will read and review the book, but I know you all intend to. Thank you all for the precious gift of your time. I hope I have not wasted it!

About the Author

Greg Leunig lives in Kansas City, Missouri with his wife and two dogs, each of whom is somehow simultaneously completely in charge. His day job involves saving the world AKA chipping away at the megalithic US coal and oil industry AKA he is a sales manager at a solar company called Zenernet. He has a Master of Fine Arts Degree in Creative Writing, despite which he prefers to write about magic and robots and explosions.

Greg's fiction and poetry have variously appeared in *Daily Science Fiction*, *Apex Magazine*, *Strange Horizons*, and others. His first novel, *Multipocalypse*, appeared in serial form on the now-defunct Jukepop Serials. Learn more about Greg's work at https://pleasefeedthesquirrels.com/.

About the Publishing Team

Nate Ragolia is a lifelong lover of science fiction and its power to imagine worlds more hopeful and inclusive than the real one. His first book, *There You Feel Free*, was published by 1888's Black Hill Press in 2015. Spaceboy Books reissued it in 2021. He's also the author of *The Retroactivist*, published by Spaceboy Books. He founded and edited *BONED*, a literary magazine, has created webcomics, and pets dogs.

Shaunn Grulkowski has been compared to Warren Ellis and Phillip K. Dick and was once described as what a baby conceived by Kurt Vonnegut and Margaret Atwood would turn out to be. He's at least the fifth best Slavic-Latino-American sci-fi writer in the Baltimore metro area. He's the author *Retcontinuum*, and the editor of *A Stalled Ox* and *The Goldfish* for 1888/Black Hill Press.